MOONLIGHT SHIFTER

MIYO HUNTER

MOONLIGHT SHIFTER

MIYO HUNTER

CONTENTS

To anyone who wondered after a harsh break up if things were going to be okay. This book is a reminder that putting your ex in the trash can is the first step to a fabulous new life

CONTENT WARNING

This book contains:
    Graphic depictions of violence.
    Kidnapping.
    Unethical Human Experimentation.
    Mature sexual situations.

If you object to violent imagery, cursing and spicy scenes, this is not the series for you.

-xoxo Miyo

CHAPTER 1
CAMILLE

I never meant to fall in love.

For your generic, garden variety human, falling in love isn't a big deal. Most people—even the worst of them—eventually find a partner. But then again, I wasn't human.

Those born with the blood of the wolf coursing through their veins often waited. When we came of age, we stood together under the light of the full moon, to see who the Goddess would choose. We waited to see if the beast would burst forth, breaking out of our human bodies. To see who among us would become shifters.

Because everyone knows that all shifters have a soulmate. Just one.

All it took was one touch, and a bond would spark into place between them. Marking them as fated mates... as destiny.

We'd all heard the warnings.

The warnings I had chosen to ignore.

Shifters avoided falling in love because of what happened to me.

THE HOWLERS' Den had music and pheromones pumping, alcohol flowing and the occasional snarls and bared fangs, as squabbles between the wolves got heated. Living with an animal inside your chest, the two best methods of getting relief, were either fighting or fucking. That's how gangs of shifter men ended up in the mixed martial arts ring downstairs, working out their aggression with their fists and claws. Or for shifters still waiting to spark with their mates, there was the option of numbing the beast with cheap booze.

My drink was watermelon and cucumber flavored, though I wasn't one of the girls waiting on fate and the old gods to tell me who to be with. I'd already found the love of my life, fate be damned. I was drinking because I felt like it, not because I had to.

It was Friday night, and I was feeling good. Looking amazing in a skin-tight leather crop top and pants that hugged all of my curves in all the right places. My lipstick was neon-berry, and I didn't need to see the longing glances following me to know that I looked utterly kissable.

Mike was going to want to eat me up as soon as I got home.

Here among my own kind, I could let loose some of the wariness that came with being among humans. The need to hold back strength and stuff down the snarls of the wolves that lived within you was a constant effort. It was a little easier on guys, but humans tended not to react well to women snarling like animals. Sexists—the lot of them.

But I wasn't completely relaxed. The dancers around me were all women as far as I could see, but I wouldn't really be able to enjoy myself unless I checked.

When I pulled on my wolf senses, the vibrant colors of the room faded to muted blues, yellows and grays. What I lost in sight, came alive in the scents in the air. The chemical tang of deodorant and perfume. The malty notes of beer, along with the sharper acetone tang of vodka. The syrupy smooth textures of rum.

There was the jumbled mess of pheromones that smelled like everything from light florals, to musty, to traces of urine.

I could smell emotions; the sweet lavender scent of oxytocin. Plenty of dopamine and serotonin also hung in the air—those smells always reminded me of baking cookies or finding the purse I'd been drooling over in the discount section.

I could smell the earthy, almost pungent scent of the wolves coiled within the bodies of the dancers.

None of that was what I was checking for.

Then the fainter scent of testosterone and cortisol, but that was further off. That concentrated masculine scent was drifting in from downstairs, mixed in with all the musty sweat, the sulfuric bite of tension. Anxiety.

There was a whiff of male on the dance floor. My gaze darted in that direction, and found a couple dancing together. A burly alpha had his arms wrapped possessively around his mate, and the two of them were swaying together, moving to the beat. As the couple's soulmarks touched, swirls of light flickered across each of their marks.

The pair of them looked deliriously happy. Which was great for them.

I had nothing to worry about from a soul mated pair.

It would have been nice to have Mike here with me tonight. Keeping an eye out for male shifters, or even just dancing with me. He'd said that he was exhausted from work, and told me to go on and have fun. Make it a girl's night.

It was nice that he trusted me, I guess.

As far as my wolf could tell, there weren't many male shifters on this floor and none were anywhere near me.

I let out a sigh, as tension I wasn't aware of loosened in my shoulders.

Releasing the senses of the wolf, colors burst across my vision like everything was in technicolor.

Surrounded by my girls, in the hottest shifter club in town, I let my hips sway to the music and let loose—without the pressure to act human or any fear of being discovered. I was completely free to be myself. Here, surrounded by my own kind.

With my drink held high in one hand, I rocked to the beat on the dance floor. I was lost to the music, eyes closed, shimmying my shoulders, moving and grooving. Singing along with the lyrics, and making up the words I didn't know.

My favorite song was playing. I finished my third drink and the alcohol was starting to kick in. I was getting wrapped up into the flow of it, riding high. Everything was all good vibes tonight.

Cheers rang out from downstairs.

Some part of my brain was ringing alarm bells. That noise was important.

But then the beat dropped, and I was banging my head with the chorus, hitting every single beat. My worries were drowning under the bubbly euphoria of the night.

Everything became more crowded for some reason,

which was making my wolf on edge. But I grooved over to the edge of the dance floor, making it look absolutely fabulous as I started my retreat.

I jerked out of the way of an aggressive dancer, with overenthusiastic swinging arms... just to find myself bumping straight into someone else. Someone hard.

One little bump should have been no problem.

It would have been no big deal, except that it happened.

The second my shoulder touched him, heat burst across my skin. Like I had brushed against an open fire rather than a man.

All it took was one touch.

My shoulder was throbbing from the contact. My skin ached as if it was being carved as light burned me. Pale blue flashes erupted from the point of contact, spiraling around my shoulder in a geometric design. Weaving a pattern across my flesh of all the different phases of the moon. As the light faded, I could see the marks in the exact place where we touched.

This was the moment wolf shifters waited for. Some of us even waited for years. For decades. The moment everyone longed for.

Everyone but me.

This mark branded into me, wasn't just pretty decoration. No. It revealed the soulbond. The man who bumped into me, wasn't just some random sweaty and burly guy who had stepped out of the fighting pits.

He was my... soulmate.

Shit.

No.

I hadn't meant to...

Usually, I was so careful.

Always watched where I was going, made sure not to get near any unfamiliar shifter men.

There were so many people around. So many of *my* people.

Everyone knew what it was. Everyone knew what had just happened. Though the music was still blasting it was as if it was muted. All the talking ceased, as the sound in the room faded to a dull murmur.

I started gasping, I couldn't help it.

My eyes were fixed on the bare chest of the man I'd bumped into, at the marks that formed, spiraling in a swirl of constellations carved into his skin. An exact match for mine.

This was the blessing of the moon goddess. A blessing that she only bestowed once...Everyone saw this. There wouldn't be any way to act like this hadn't happened.

There was no way.

I stood frozen, staring at the man who I'd sparked with; he was large. With a body that screamed alpha. I could feel the dominance radiating from him. He wasn't just any alpha, he had the dominance of *the* alpha of a pack.

He was tall, towering over me, even in my four inch stilettos. Wavy hair and a boxer's physique—lean muscle and chiseled abs, now with that soulmark tattooed across his chest. His dark green eyes were like the undergrowth of a forest with pupils wide and locked on me.

I couldn't do this. I couldn't be here.

I did the only thing I could.

I spun hard on my stiletto heels and ran.

CHAPTER 2
ROMAN

The fighting ring was my only outlet—the only place where I could let go of the mantle of alpha. I was responsible for an entire pack that had been wasted away by the war, with our numbers dwindling dangerously low.

Walking out of the fighting pit, all the tension that I wore was loosened. I wasn't as stretched tight anymore with the constant need to keep everyone safe. I'd released some of the stress that I was as accustomed to wearing as a second skin.

I wasn't wary enough when one of the pretty dancers knocked straight into my path.

The moment that I felt the soulbond spark across my chest, I blanched at my first immediate reaction.

Fuck, I don't have time for a mate.

The second that the thoughts were out of my head, I tried to reign them back in. I meant no disrespect to the moon goddess. If she meant for me to have a mate, I would take on that responsibility as well.

That wasn't fair to her. It wasn't this girl's fault that the

Blackwood pack had been decimated by war. That she had just been matched to an alpha who had to rebuild the entire pack structure from the ground up.

Like the packs on surrounding territories our numbers had dropped drastically.

It wasn't even our fucking war.

Over the years, my pack had simply gotten pulled into the violence. Who even knew why the two packs were fighting anymore? Some territorial or cultural dispute that had blown up and lasted for centuries.

Yet the war alone couldn't account for the loss in our numbers.

Something had happened to our wolves.

Our numbers had fallen drastically under the replacement levels.

Unlike other packs, we didn't have the manpower to fix this. To maintain our infrastructure.

None of the previous alphas took adequate records. I'd inherited this mess five years ago, and I could already tell that something wasn't adding up with the number of shifter births and the number of wolves we currently had.

Some of the shifters had vanished. Seemingly without a trace.

Everything in our pack had to be modernized. Everything from the plumbing, to the electricity in our pack house was a decade overdue for maintenance. Our numbers were too low to put in the kind of money needed for those major repairs. Everything was held together by duct tape and pure stubbornness.

The other packs were willing to live in the past. Some more than others. I think that there wasn't a single member of the Stonevalley pack that even owned a cell phone.

Walking into their territory was like walking directly into a pocket of the past.

It made it nearly impossible to make any kind of treaty agreements with them.

All of those thoughts fell out of my head like water pouring through a sieve the moment I glanced at my soulmate.

Holy Shit.

She was gorgeous.

She was more than gorgeous.

The girl looked ethereal, and more luscious than anything I'd imagined in my wildest dreams. She was dressed all in all tight leather. Sexy, with a dark edge, something wild brimming in the depths of her lovely eyes. There was strength that shone in her violet eyes, brimming like fire just below the surface.

I stared, dazed. In awe that someone so lovely, so fierce, could be the other half of my soul. For one moment, my heart was racing, and euphoria pounded through my veins. Goddess above, she was beautiful.

Then she took one look at the soul marks that bloomed across our skin. One look at me. Admittedly, I hadn't been looking my best. I'd just gotten out of the fighting ring, and my eye was swelling. My knuckles were bruised, and I'm pretty sure I stank like adrenaline. Obviously I looked better than the other guy, but still. Not the way I'd imagined meeting my soulmate for the first time.

She'd taken one look at me and turned pale. Before I could say a single word, she turned and ran, sprinting straight out of the club as if she'd been terrified that I was going to hunt her down.

I stood absolutely floored.

The club was quiet. Even the harsh beat of the music

seemed muted. Nothing was louder than the harsh clack of her heels clacking against the dance floor as she ran.

More than the humiliation that burned through me, was a heavy dose of shock. Grief.

My soulmate... rejected me. Before I could even say a single word to her.

"Should I follow? Alpha?"

I could smell the sharp acid stench of anger in the air. My generals were furious. Furious to see their alpha disrespected in such a manner.

I couldn't blame them. I would have felt the same, before I had taken on the mantle of authority in my pack. If I'd seen a slight to my alpha, I wouldn't allow that to go unchallenged.

But that was before I saw the expression on her lovely face.

My soulmate looked terrified.

Of bonding?

Of me?

I'd never spoken a word to the girl, couldn't even recognize her. There was no way that I would be able to see a face and figure like hers and not remember her. No, she didn't know me. Yet for some reason, I terrified her.

The brief look of fear on her face was enough for me to cool my own hurt.

"Follow her," at my command, Nyx looked ready to bare his fangs. Full on hunt her down. I stopped him with a sharp growl. "*Just* follow. Don't approach her. I want to know who she is."

CHAPTER 3
CAMILLE

As soon as I got in the front door, I flung both of my arms around Mike, pulling him close as I pressed a desperate kiss against his lips.

"What's gotten into you all of a sudden?" Mike chuckled, pressing his forehead against mine. Close enough that our exhales intermingled. Close enough to breathe him in —the familiar scent of patchouli and citrus of the man I'd chosen.

He smelled like home. Like the earthy scent of the forest on a rainy day. Like the mint of his toothpaste. Like the faint traces of the spices that he'd cooked in the lunch that he'd made for me.

Rather than answering him, I growled. Ripping at his shirt hard enough that buttons had gone flying.

"Oh, fuck yeah," he snarled in reply, as he grabbed at my leather crop top and yanked it up, exposing my tits. I had a jacket on, hiding the soulmark on my shoulder, but luckily I'd already managed to distract him enough that he didn't bother to remove it. He lifted me onto our kitchen counter, stepping in-between my parted thighs, pressing close enough for me to feel the exact shape of his cock, right where I needed it.

Mike caressed familiar patterns down my sides, feeling along the undersides of my breasts, until his hands moved to my hips. He tugged my leather leggings down to my knees, before scrambling to unbuckle his belt, freeing himself. He didn't even bother to take off my panties, just pushed them out of the way before roughly plunging into me.

Making every inch of my body alight.

It was almost enough to help me forget the anxiety of my wolf.

Usually, whenever I was with Mike, my wolf was silent for the entire affair.

As soon as Mike pressed himself inside of me, I could feel my wolf begin to whine.

It was the first sound that she'd made in hours. My wolf had gone quiet after I'd run from my soulmate. I'd had to fight against her every step that I'd taken away from the Howlers' Den. My wolf couldn't understand what I'd done.

I felt her presence in the back of my mind as Mike moved within me, slamming into me hard.

She was antsy, acting as if danger was near. Louder than Mike's groans of pleasure, I could hear my wolf panting. Anxious.

This wasn't at all close to the first time I'd slept with Mike. She'd never complained about getting laid before.

I ignored her.

Instead, I focused on the pleasure. Mike groaned, moving faster as he always did as he got close to finishing. Abruptly he pulled out of me, gripping himself and tugging his member with rapid strokes that almost looked painful.

My heart sank a little as Mike jerked himself off,

harshly. It just felt incomplete, ending out lovemaking this way—like something was missing.

He groaned as he came in fat spurts across my stomach.

Mike panted as he caught his breath, before patting my thigh affectionately.

"Hey Mike, next time do you think you could finish... in me?" I understood why he'd been hesitant in the past, with the threat of finding our mates hanging over us. Maybe he would realize that things were different now. After all, we'd been together for years.

But Mike just shook his head.

"Cami, you know we can't risk it."

He handed me some dry paper towels before heading off to the bathroom to clean up.

Leaving me alone with the wolf who had gone silent within me once more. As if she was judging me.

This is nothing like how the others had described the wild claiming between wolves.

I shoved that feeling far down. Smothering it away.

I'd chosen this. I'd chosen this man.

The two of us, we were more than our fates.

Why should I end up with someone because of some biological imperative? Because the moon goddess had decided that some other alpha would be the best candidate for strong offspring?

No.

That wasn't good enough for me.

Mike and I had made promises to one another. We loved each other.

That was more important than our biology.

I loved him with all the years we had grown up together.

Within my chest, my wolf whined.

CHAPTER 4
ROMAN

I stopped pulling my punches in the fighting ring.

I knew that I had a problem. Knew it every time I looked into my opponents eyes and could see them try to hide a wince. There were too many broken bones and bashed skulls.

Some days in the ring, I'd let myself cut it too close. Let the rage take over and go a little too far. My generals once had to hurl themselves into the fighting pits and pull me off some shifter who was only hanging on to life by a thread.

In every other aspect of my life, I held it together, diving deep into my responsibilities. I'd actually made a decent headway with the renovation project for the communal pack kitchen.

The kitchen's plumbing and outdated refrigerator units and stoves were a common concern that pack members had brought to my attention. Using the bulk of my winnings in the ring helped me to hire a decent construction company. They had already installed some new appliances and torn down a water damaged wall.

I wasn't turning into a complete animal.

Tonight, it felt a little easier to pull myself off my opponent once he'd gone unconscious. I slipped under the ropes and down the raised platform of the ring, ignoring the half-hearted and scattered applause.

Either I needed another outlet to work out my aggression, or I was going to wear out my welcome at Howlers. Grabbing my towel, I sat down to scrub the mix of blood and sweat off my knuckles.

Nyx sat down at my side, casually, the picture of calm; only the bouncing of his foot and the faint acid scent of anxiety showed that he was anything but. Not that I would say a word to stop him, but I already could tell that I wasn't going to like this. I was well aware that I needed an intervention, but that did nothing to quiet the haze of rage that was threatening to drown me.

Nyx bent his head, respectfully. "Have you considered having a talk with the Evenfall Ridge alpha?"

My hands froze right in the middle of scrubbing blood. The Evenfall Ridge alpha was the alpha of my soulmate's pack.

Camille.

I'd learned a lot about my soulmate in the past few weeks, despite never speaking to her a single time.

Though she was a member, she had been in low contact with the rest of the Ridges for years. It had something to do with a family dispute with her father, who was a high ranking alpha in the pack, and someone she was actively trying to avoid. Camille never joined any of the pack affairs. Never ran with the other wolves during the full moon. She didn't have an official job within the pack, or seem to benefit at all from the community. It was as if she was a lone wolf living within the territory.

But despite her low engagement in the pack, she was

still a member. If her alpha gave an order, she would be bound to it. I knew Simon, the Evenfall Ridge's alpha, personally. Even had his number in my phone contacts. It wouldn't be hard at all to persuade him. If he ordered Camille to join my pack, she would be forced to submit to his authority. She would be forced to obey her alpha's commands or else be banished from his territory.

It was an impossible choice for her to make. There was only one thing holding her to that pack. I'd already seen his picture.

"No," my tone left no room for argument.

I could still feel the echoes of it. The flutter of her climaxing through the bond. It was almost enough for me to want to rip out our connection at the root, and tear it out of me. Every time I felt her take her pleasure with another man, it made my wolf go absolutely feral. Feeling her satisfaction burning through the soulmark on my chest... so close... as if it happened right under my skin—it made my wolf claw at my flesh. Tearing into my ribs, gnashing and shredding through muscle trying to force his way out of me. It took every last ounce of my willpower to reign in the wolf —if I let up for just a moment and let the wolf out, I wouldn't be able to stop him until his teeth were sunk deep into that man's throat. Biting down hard. Enough to rip straight through the vulnerable skin and muscle, and severing down to the bone.

I knew everything there was to know about her lover.
Mike Bowman.

The only son of an old gamma wolf, who had a job in the pack for the past two centuries as a repair-man. He was following in his old man's footsteps, fixing small appliances for his pack. He'd been in a relationship with my mate for years. Apparently the two of them had been together since high school.

All I needed to do was say the words. It would take me less than a minute to type out a text message to Simon, and Camille would be delivered to me in less than a day.

I'd never do that to her. I would never force my soulmate to come to me. No matter how desperately my wolf fought me, this was out of my hands.

"Are you sure you don't want—"

I shook my head.

"How is she?" My wolf was heated, and the fighting pits weren't enough. The only thing that soothed him were these reports. Hearing that she was safe was the only thing holding him back from charging into enemy territory after her.

"Her wolf has been rather on edge, but the girl has been spending a good deal of time as a human."

I nodded. Her wolf wasn't happy either to be forced from her mate. But Camille was choosing to deal with it, so I would have to do the same.

"Don't get too close. I don't want her to know that she's being watched." It was all I could do.

She was the other half of my soul, but she wasn't mine.

CHAPTER 5
CAMILLE

My heart raced whenever I went out of the house. For the past few weeks, I'd looked over my shoulder, certain to see my mate in the shadows, coming for me.

I didn't even know his name...

Even without his name, his face was embedded into my memory like a tattoo directly on my brain. I could perfectly picture the look on his face, the intensity in his expression. Every inch of that shifter radiated authority. He stank of alpha power. The kind of dominance that sunk all the way into your skin and settled into your bones. Taking over from the root. I knew from experience how very dominant wolves could be when things didn't go their way.

More than anything I could see his dark green eyes, wild like the forest, with pupils wide and locked on me. He looked ready to devour me.

He was nothing like the mate that I had chosen for myself. As the son of a gamma wolf, Mike was just as strong as I needed him to be—without all the rank and status and all of the hierarchy drama that so many of the other wolves seemed to thrive on. I didn't bother to bring up the sparking incident with Mike. I just pretended like nothing happened.

He didn't say anything about the fact that I had started wearing thin sweaters over my shoulders, even though that had never been my style. But he had given my new outfit choice a weird look. It was the summer after all, and I'd never been ashamed of my body. Had never chosen to hide it.

Later that day, I stopped by the store after working my shift, and picked up three bottles of cover-up foundation. It only took an extra five minutes or so to completely cover my mark. Then the thin sweaters became a thing of the past, and I could walk around in whatever I wanted.

Obviously I was never going to go back to the Howlers' Den. Yes, I'd have to avoid shifter clubs for a while. Maybe forever. Until I could figure out how I was going to talk to Mike about this.

This isn't fair to your soulmate. You just rejected him without even giving him a reason...

I shoved that thought down ruthlessly.

Never once in my life had I asked to have a soulmate. It wasn't fair.

I'd made no promises to the man. I never agreed to be in a relationship with him.

It wasn't fair of anyone to expect me to drop everything and devote myself to a stranger. Why should I? Just because it was socially acceptable? Because of peer pressure? As far as I was concerned there was no goddess, no magical bonding event that could tell me that I had to devote myself to a man.

As the weeks marched by, my life settled into a new normal. A normal where I was no longer free to party at all the shifter clubs I used to love.

Some of my friends (okay fine, almost all of them) stopped returning my calls and texts.

It made sense. I had to stop going out with them.

Your friends are all waiting for their mates. They are probably pissed at you for throwing yours away.

If those were the kind of friends I had, I didn't need them. I didn't need people around me who were just going to judge me. I could do it all on my own. Far from their judgment.

If my mother was still alive to see this, what would she say about her only daughter giving up on her soulmate?

If my mother wasn't so hopelessly devoted to her joke of a soulmate, maybe she'd be alive to see this.

Wherever she was, looking down on me, mother just wanted me to be happy. Yes, my mother was traditional, but I'm sure that I would have been able to sit her down to talk to her. Explain to her what I was doing with Mike. She would have understood. Besides, not every shifter mate works out.

My own parents were proof of that.

They never should have been together.

I think that my father was happier with a mate of his choosing. Not that I was certain about that. I hadn't spoken to the man in almost a decade.

The isolation was chafing, but I still had Mike, and he made all of this worth it.

Even though I never said a word about the incident to anyone, it almost seemed to me like Mike had become more distant after I sparked with my soulmate.

He wouldn't talk to me about it, and said that everything was fine whenever I asked.

I noticed that he had started to cloak his scent in clove oil so that my wolf wouldn't be able to pick up on his emotions. It made me feel more distant from him. I couldn't even soothe myself with his familiar scent.

It was possible that we had let things get stale after being together for so long. It's not like we were the only couple in a long term relationship that got too comfortable. It was something we just needed to keep an eye on, but we could manage it.

Mike was my first boyfriend, he was my first *everything*. The two of us had grown up together. He'd been my friend, before we were ever lovers. My absolute rock over the years. How would I have gotten through the death of my mother? The decision to go no contact with my father and low contact with my pack? I never would have been able to get out of that toxic environment without him.

It was almost as if he knew somehow about the whole sparking incident.

But how could he...

No.

What if somebody told him? There were so many shifters at the club, all of my friends knew who I was dating.

If he knew I had found my soulmate... what would he think? That I just caved and gave in to the moon goddess? That after everything the two of us had been through, that

I'd just start messing around with another man and pretend like everything was normal?

He couldn't think that just because I found my soulmate that meant I would cheat on him?

Even though I hadn't done anything wrong... after all the times that I'd told Mike that I never wanted a soulmate of my own. What if he just didn't believe me?

Mike must have heard what was going on, must have made his own assumptions.

Well, then, I'd just have to clear the air. Our anniversary was just a week away, it was the perfect time for us to reconnect. For me to come clean about the soulbond, and make it clear that I had never wanted it.

I was going to prove to him that he had nothing to worry about from my soulmate.

CHAPTER 6
CAMILLE

Stretching out across the cool sheets, I groggily reached out to my lover, wanting to snuggle into his warmth. With my eyes closed, I frowned patting around his side of the bed and feeling nothing but smooth satin. There was not a single trace of warmth left. I stubbornly patted his side of the bed, before blearily opening one eye.

Mike was gone.

By the faint trace of his lingering scent, he'd been gone for quite some time.

It was the morning of our five year anniversary, and Mike wasn't even around—he'd gone in for work.

I rolled over to my night stand, and grabbed my phone off the charger. There was no text message, not even a single emoji.

Did he really just leave without a single text?

It was six in the morning, a little early for him to have left for work. It was odd that he hadn't even mentioned anything over dinner the night before.

For our third anniversary, Mike had gotten us a hotel

reservation, with fancy bottle service. Last year he'd woken me with a dozen silver roses—for the color of my wolf—his kisses over every inch of me, and a morning of hot sex.

But just leaving as if today meant nothing... this wasn't like him.

Could he be planning a surprise or something?

That wasn't his usual style. But there was no way that he had forgotten. I couldn't believe that.

Whatever it meant, this gave me time to make my own plans. Everything was going to be perfect for tonight.

I WENT into one of the human malls, after making sure that there wasn't another shifter in sight. I headed straight for what the humans did best: having a product for everything. In this case, I was looking for a reminder of how much my lover meant to me.

Malls were tough on my shifter senses.

The younger the shifter the easier it was to separate the human senses from the wolf. But for older shifters it became harder to make the distinction between the two.

Some of the older wolves were able to live far past a regular human life span. It had something to do with how the process of shifting broke apart the body, to release the wolf. Making the transition back to human was like a hard reset on the body. Wolves were pulled straight back to a moment in time in our DNA. Though some of the wolves died in the fights and in the wars, it wasn't at all uncommon for wolves to live far beyond a normal human lifespan. I've met shifters who I thought were just a decade or so older than me and later realized that I was off. By several hundred years.

For much older shifters, coming to a human mall would be like having any other wild animal in a confined space. Too many sounds, too many sensations all pressed in too close.

I was still new enough to shifting that I was still able to slip into the human world undetected, without it being obvious that there was something different about me. Something other.

It was starting to get harder for me to be in such a crowded human space. I swear, it becomes harder every year.

A baby was crying. There were too many footsteps from too many people echoing around the high mall ceiling. Impossible to track where any of them were going. If I focused a little harder with my sensitive wolf hearing, it would sound like a stampede.

In my human form, my sense of smell was only slightly elevated, but here in the mall the smells were overpowering. There was too much. All the different types of grease wafting together in the air from the food court. Salt and oil. Cheese pumped full of chemicals. Grilled onion mixed with the scent of people's deodorants and strong perfumes. It was all a jumble in my mind. Enough to give me a headache.

I was already overstimulated by the time I got to the bold pink neon lights and the mannequins sporting huge feathered wings. Bingo.

It was a lingerie store, I forgot the name. Somebody's Secret.

But I'd been here before, and the result was completely

worth it. I couldn't wait to see Mike's eyes bulge out of his head once he got a chance to unwrap me like a present.

The store was filled with all of the usual lace ensembles, which would have had me blushing all the way to my ears the first time I'd shopped here. But now that I had a bit of experience under my belt, the lace seemed a little too... basic.

I wandered through the displays, trying to find something that was just the right level of spicy. There were pretty floral pieces, and a nice little red number. But there was nothing that really screamed *me.* I wanted to pick something that would remind Mike exactly how good the two of us could be together.

Behind another weird statue of a headless woman who had wings for some reason (I mean that wasn't supposed to be some kind of shifter was it? I'd never even heard of a human who shifted into a creature with wings. Just plenty of wolves, and the occasional bear, at least that I'd seen). There was a leather corset, with cutouts in all the right places. I could just picture it on my body, it looked like it was made for me—sexy with a dark edge. With a hint of something wild beneath the surface. It was perfect. The tag was hidden just inside, and I winced as soon as I saw the price, *one hundred and eighty dollars? Really?*

But this was our anniversary. What kind of price could you put on five years?

It would put a dent in my savings, but I could always build those back up. What better time was it than now to seize the moment? I'd bring back those feelings and remind Mike exactly why he'd fallen in love with me in the first place.

With my purchase secured, I got out of the mall.

It was too bad. I'd only gone to one store before being

overstimulated. When I'd only just shifted for the first time, I'd still been able to go shopping for an entire day. With the passing of time, the part of me that was a human was beginning to fade somewhat.

On the way home, I picked up a bottle of our favorite wine and some ingredients for dinner. Even though it was obvious that I was going to be the main meal on the platter, I was also pulling together some of our favorites for a romantic meal. My pan seared sirloin steak with creamy mashed potatoes topped with sauteed mushrooms was enough to put anyone in the mood.

As soon as I got home, I tried on the corset and it fit like a dream. Just like I knew it would. The leather hugged every one of my curves. The cut outs provided the perfect little hint of everything Mike could be missing out on. All he would have to do was reach out for what we had, and I was his for the taking. He could unwrap me like a present and dive right in.

As soon as I got the lingerie on, I knew that it wasn't coming off. Not unless it was Mike ripping it off with his teeth. So instead I found a long trench coat and wrapped myself up in it and got to work. Hey, the lingerie wasn't coming off, but I wasn't dumb enough to cook with that much skin exposed.

It was a little early to start cooking, but I wanted to get everything done early so I'd have time to set the mood. Pulling out all the stops, tonight we'd dine with fancy plates and scented candles. Mike wasn't supposed to come home for a couple of hours still, and he wouldn't expect me home until even later in the evening. My boss was fairly flexible with me and had given me the night off when I'd explained that it was our anniversary. It was the perfect opportunity to surprise him.

I threw butter in the pan, setting the burner to run red hot. I watched as the meat sizzled and the nice bits of juicy steak browned up perfectly. I pulled out one for me a few minutes earlier. Mike liked to have his steak well done.

Crushing the potatoes took a little bit of effort on my part, as I deliberately had to hold back my wolf, who was strong enough to crush the pot itself, to say nothing of the potatoes within it. She was agitated, like she had been since that night in the club, but I'd managed to use enough restraint that the potatoes came out whipped and airy. I didn't even put a single dent into the pot.

I plated up the steaks and mashed potatoes with the browned mushrooms. The smell of our meal was perfection, I couldn't—

The door handle jostled. *Shit.*

It was earlier than I'd anticipated—a full hour before Mike's usual time home from work. I hadn't even lit the candles yet.

Did I have time to reveal my lingerie? I toyed with the jacket, pulling open the top three buttons to reveal a generous amount of cleavage.

If I managed to distract my man, the food would go cold, but it would all be worth it.

The door swung open and Mike walked in.

That look on his face—there it was—there was the Mike I knew and loved. He had a smile that was so genuine it warmed all the way through me. He had a laugh on the tip of his lips, and a smile that shone in his eyes. Until all I could feel was the exuberance of it.

But then he noticed me looking hopefully at him, and the smile froze off his face, before disappearing entirely.

What? What was he?

"Shit. You're early." Mike sighed.

What the hell did he mean by that?

There was a thick tension in the air, nagging at me. Something that set my teeth on edge, and had my wolf on immediate alert.

Then, as if I was hit over the head with it, I detected an unexpected scent through the aroma of steak and wine, even over the faint traces of clove that usually hung on Mike's clothes. A scent that was completely foreign.

He was standing there, practically bathed in another woman's sugary tangerine scent, so strongly that he reeked of it.

Why the hell did he smell like another woman?

Shadows lingered beneath Mike's eyes as if they were hooded with secrets.

"I didn't mean for you to find out like this."

CHAPTER 7
CAMILLE

I clenched my hands at my sides to stop them from shaking.

What was going on? There had to be a reasonable explanation for this.

"Camille," Mike sighed, and that's when I got scared.

He never called me Camille. I was always Cami, or Baby, or Gorgeous. When was the last time that Mike called me by my first name?

A pit opened in the bottom of my stomach.

I told it to go away.

It didn't go.

He strode across the kitchen, not glancing once at the steak dinner I'd plated for the two of us. Not even taking a single peek at my cleavage. Once he'd crossed through the kitchen, without turning to face me, he called out, "There's something I have to show you."

I couldn't even look at the plastic shopping bag filled with candles, stuffed hastily on the kitchen chair, just out of sight. I wasn't even sure exactly what was happening, but suddenly I wanted to take that bag and jam it straight into the trash. I didn't even know what was going on, just that a part of me wanted to jump out of my skin and that everything had gone wrong somehow.

What the hell was happening? Maybe if I'd had time to light the candles, or if I had managed to remove my coat and show off the lovely new lingerie I'd bought...

I shook my head, steadying myself. Something told me that whatever this was, it wasn't something that could be fixed with candles or underwear. Not even the expensive kind.

Numb. My heart pounding so hard the only thing I could hear was the beat drumming in my ear, I followed him. Mike didn't stop until he got to the bathroom.

Had he found my concealer make up? Did he realize that I'd met my soulmate?

I never meant to meet my soulmate, and even though I did, it didn't mean anything to me. I would never break the promises we made to one another... Wait. My stomach dropped all the way to the floor. Did he think I'd *cheated* on him?

Was that what this past month was all about? I would never do something like that to him. I love him. Mike knew that I love him. Right?

But Mike didn't reach into the back of the cupboards where I'd hidden my skin products and the concealer. Instead he flipped on the sink faucet, and placed his hands under the water.

It was like my brain turned to static. I watched as the foundation washed away, dripping down his fingers, coloring the sink in his warm skin tones. The scent of the make up was the only thing in the air, no longer hidden by the strong essence of clove he'd started wearing. Once he'd removed all of the makeup, I could see his soulmark. The dainty dips and swirls of constellations. Phases of the moon in a pattern that didn't match my own mark. It looked nothing like the one I'd kept hidden on my shoulder.

Okay...

Mike wasn't my soulmate, I'd always known that. From the moment I'd touched him after my first shift, I'd known that he wasn't the one that fate decided for me. But he was still my chosen mate.

This didn't change anything.

So why was the look on his face so devastated?

"I met my soulmate, Camille. I can't keep doing this with you."

He was speaking to me, but for some reason it was like I couldn't understand the words that he was saying.

What was happening?

"Mike?"

"It happened a few months back. I just didn't know how to tell you."

"We said that we would reject our soulmates."

Mike shook his head slowly. Like I was some hopeless idiot for reciting back the words that we had literally spoken to one another a thousand times.

We had promised one another that we wouldn't try to find our soulmates. That even if we found them, we would reject them.

Just because fate had placed its mark on some other girl, none of that erased the five years that we had...

Mike let out a heavy sigh. "She's pregnant."

Mike's mouth was still moving, but I couldn't hear a word that he said. All I heard was a harsh ringing in my ears.

"What?" The word slipped out of my mouth without my permission.

Mike blinked at me, ruefully.

I recognized that look on his face, though I never imagined that it would be directed at me.

It was pity.

"I said. I'm going to need you to move out of here."

I just stared at him.

"I'm sorry." Mike was just shaking his head. "But your name isn't on the lease. My mate's been having a tough pregnancy. I need to be there for her."

I couldn't quite wrap my head around everything that was happening.

He wanted me to leave? Where was I supposed to go? I didn't make enough money to pay for rent on my own. If I'd had some time to prepare I could have saved for a deposit...

Wait... he was breaking up with me?

The smell of the other woman... that was his mate?

How long had—did I even want to know how long this had been going on for? At least as long as it took to make a baby. Shifter women tended to have a hard time conceiving. There was no way this woman would have gotten pregnant from a one time thing. But Mike and I had just slept together three days ago... Didn't it take at least two weeks for women to know they were pregnant?

Angry tears welled up in the corner of my eyes, blurring my vision, and I scrubbed them away furiously. This had to be a mistake. None of this was happening. Mike wouldn't... He wouldn't do this to me.

"Oh come on, Camille. Don't fucking cry." Mike's face was twisted into something angry. Into someone I didn't even recognize anymore. As if it was *I* who had done something awful to *him*. "I'm not a human. You can't put that on me. What the two of us were doing, we were acting like humans. It was driving my wolf absolutely nuts."

Anything logical that I might have wanted to say, about the lease, about having to find a new job—I couldn't say, I couldn't even think straight. For some reason, all I could think about was that little plastic bag full of candles I'd bought for our anniversary. Their scent was oakmoss and it reminded me of the first time we ran through the woods together. As humans, not as wolves. Sneaking out together. Giving in to our attraction. The rain was heavy that day, but it was like we hadn't even felt it. We were completely lost in one another. Then maybe it was Mike who'd leaned in. Or maybe it was me, but then the next thing I knew, his mouth was pressed against mine, sending fireworks skittering down my spine.

"But we promised..." The words slipped out. As soon as they were out of my mouth, all small and pathetic, I wanted to shove the words back inside.

"Camille," He said my name like it was a curse word. Like the two of us had never been in love at all. Mike wasn't even looking at me anymore. "We were kids. At some point, you gotta just grow the fuck up."

My entire world was shattering all around me, and Mike... the man I loved, the man who had been my first everything... first dance. First kiss. Now I guess my first heartbreak too. He'd promised that he was always going to be there for me. How could he do this to me? He was staring at me as if I was nothing more to him than an inconvenience.

I stared at him blankly.

I should be feeling something. Anger. Rage. Because he'd cheated on me. He'd gotten another woman pregnant, after he'd promised that he'd have to be crazy to even think about touching anyone but me.

Mike and I had grown up together. He'd always been

my staunch defender. He'd always encouraged me to be myself. Always given me the love and grace that I needed in order to flourish, even when everything had blown up with my dad. When the rest of the pack had practically turned their backs on me, Mike had been my rock.

Who the hell was this man? Blaming me for our breakup. Calling me childish.

Breakup?

What the hell was happening? Was this really real?

It felt like the world was spinning around my head as if I was drunk. Like I was spiraling. Everything was moving all around me, and I was the one frozen in place.

When we were just thirteen years old, I remember Mike sitting behind me and casually grabbing my hand, caressing my fingers when I handed papers back to him in school.

How he would stare at me, like I was the only girl who existed. I was firmly at the center of his world.

I wanted to whisper no. That he couldn't do this. Not on our anniversary. The one he'd obviously forgotten.

But what did it matter that it was our anniversary? We don't have a relationship anymore. All that it measured is how much time we spent locked up in this stupid delusion together. Time that was now just wasted.

With the way he was treating me now... and if I was being perfectly honest, for a while now, things hadn't been right between us. He'd been treating me coldly long before I'd bumped into my soulmate. That was just the moment I'd let myself first notice it.

"I'm going to leave to let you process everything. But Camille, when I come back, I need you to be gone." Mike walked past me without a second glance, as if he hadn't just emotionally eviscerated me. No final words about what these last five years had meant to him.

I guess maybe they hadn't meant anything after all.

He was already out the door. Already walking down the hallway out of the apartment. Getting further and further away from me.

That didn't matter. With my wolf senses, I could hear him dialing a number on his cellphone as clearly as if he was in the same room as me.

"Yeah, I did it... I'm so sorry it took so long, Baby."

Mike laughed at something the other woman said. I knew him well enough to be able to perfectly picture his expression. It was the same laugh he'd shared so often with me. The laugh he saved when he was making fun of someone else.

"I'm on my way back. Love you, Baby."

CHAPTER 8
CAMILLE

I carved another bite of the steak, now working on the one that was supposed to be for Mike. I'd already polished off my own.

I had no appetite, but I'd be damned if I left behind something that I'd prepared with so much love and care. What else was I going to do? Throw it in the trash? Leave it behind in the fridge for the new woman to enjoy?

Honestly, I had other priorities right now. I had to reorient my life around this new reality.

Yeah, my name wasn't on the lease, but I split the rent payments with him, and I'd already paid my share for this month. If Mike was a decent person he would at least pay me back for the three weeks left this month. But now, I realized that ship had sailed.

As soon as the last bite of steak hit my tongue, I slammed the fork down onto my plate, chewing angrily.

What the fuck was I going to do?

The thought cooled some of the heat that pounded through my veins. I couldn't stay here. Moreover, I didn't want to. This place had been my home for years, the first place where I'd felt free. I'd decorated the inside of the drawers with a vinyl print. I'd worked out a deal with the landlord, taking off part of the rent for the new countertops I'd chosen and installed. I had spent hours keeping those countertops spotless. Not even letting a single fingerprint smudge the pristine white quartz. And I'd done it all for what?

Everything I'd loved in this home was now poison to me.

Obviously, I should have put more effort into putting my hard earned money into an emergency savings account. It was just that I'd never thought I would need it. I thought that my mate... no. Not my mate. I had to remember that Mike wasn't my mate. It was just that... I never thought he'd do this to me.

Even the money that he legitimately owed me for rent, I couldn't think of getting it back from him. I didn't want anything from him. Didn't want to ever see him again—how could he do this to me?

Shit. I had to focus. Not dwell on the fact that Mike wasn't who I'd thought he was. What was I going to do? I had to face the facts—I didn't have enough money to pay for a deposit on a new apartment. Not only could I not pay for something like our one bedroom apartment on my own, there was also no way that I could pay for a shitty apartment either. Not a studio. Not even a shitty and only partially legal room tucked away in someone's attic. Not here, so close to downtown.

But then again, why should I stay?

This whole pack was a prison. I'd avoided every pack event, the runs during the full moon. The dances and celebrations. I hadn't gone to any of that in years. Being around all those other wolves would mean having to be in the vicinity of my father. After all this time, even picking up his scent made my stomach twist into knots. No. The only reason I'd stayed here was for Mike.

It turned out, that wasn't a good enough reason after all.

I went into our bedroom—not ours—just the bedroom now, and grabbed my duffel bag. The bag was all rugged canvas and built to last. It was one of the few bags I'd ever found that had a strap that would fit around my wolf.

This wasn't the first time I'd packed my entire life away into this bag.

In it went all of my favorite clothes. I wouldn't be able to bring most of my wardrobe. I carefully folded my best jeans. My favorite shirts. Mike had made the decision process a little easier. I left behind anything that reminded me of him.

I didn't have too many knick knacks. Well, I did. The stuffed silver wolf... that Mike had won for me at the fair. Obviously that wasn't coming with me. Looking through all of my things... discarding everything that he'd given me, or reminded me of the many moments we had shared together... it made it blatantly obvious how much of my life had been wrapped up in him. There was so little left... but then again, I knew from experience the importance of packing light.

The only thing that I had left was a photo of my mother that I slipped carefully into an inner pocket. That and my necessities—at least the expensive ones. Anything that I wouldn't need right away, or was easy enough to replace, didn't make the cut.

Once everything was packed, I yanked the bedroom window open, inhaling the fresh night air. I squashed the part of me that was crying out for the only place that had felt like home in my entire adult life. That was the part of me that had gotten too comfortable. Too human. In the years I'd spent here, I'd allowed myself to get soft. I'd forgotten what I truly am.

My trench coat had to go. How could I ever wear it again without thinking about the things he had just said to me? I tossed it carelessly back at the closet, where it landed on my pile of rejected clothes. Stripping out of my gorgeous lingerie, I hesitated. It wasn't like Mike had tainted it, like all the rest. He'd never even seen me in this little number. Besides, it rolled up small, and after I'd cut off all the tags was non returnable. I shoved it into the corner of the bag, zipping it with finality.

Around my neck, I buckled an obnoxiously pink dog collar. It hung loosely, like a necklace. Up close there was no denying what my wolf was. But from a distance, with the neon pink collar around my neck, most people would think twice. Maybe I was just a rather large German Shepherd? Their confusion usually lasted long enough for me to get away.

I hadn't done this in a while. It was going to hurt like a bitch.

I reached down within myself to my wolf. I'd been avoiding her. From the moment I'd first sparked a soul-bond, I'd pushed her away. Afraid that if I let her take the reins that she would turn her back on the man I'd chosen. Force me to be the mate to a man I didn't even know.

I could feel my wolf chomping at the bit, jumping up and down, rattling my rib cage, excited as a pup. If I could see her, she would be wagging her tail frantically.

Pushing her away had been my second mistake. I never should have turned my back on the wolf within me. She was strong, and gorgeous and had never let me down. Of course, my first mistake was trusting Mike in the first place. Looking back it was obvious that something had been off. I just hadn't wanted to see it... did I force myself not to notice? Did I let myself become weak... for him?

I reached down within myself to that fiercest part of myself, calling to my wolf. I felt her howling back in reply.

Without warning, all the skin from my lips to my cheeks pierced open, as a wolf jaw ripped its way through. Claws burst through my fingertips, as the bone in my thumbs snapped, moving higher. I fell to the floor on all fours, as the bones in my pelvis and spine shifted. My skin prickled, as silvery fur sprouted across every inch of my skin.

My gorgeous wolf shook herself. With the motion of it, I felt like all the stress was flung away from my body along with some loose strands of fur and wolfy drool. All that tension my human body was holding rolled off my wolf with ease.

She hopped over to my bag, obediently tugging the strap over herself, and bearing the weight gamely. Internally I winced, should I have cut down harder on the weight? If I slowed her down, it would be dangerous for her... My wolf snorted, pointing her snout into the air. If she was human she would be rolling her eyes at me.

My gorgeous silky wolf paused at the corner of the bed. The sheets had our scents mixed together... from all those hours we'd spent sweating over each other, lost in pleasure. They had a high-thread count... I'd waited for weeks for them to go on sale. I'd worked for hours at the shop to buy these and so many other things in this apartment. She lifted one hind leg, carefully aiming...

My human side stirred from within the wolf. About to pull back the reins. Put a stop to this, but then settled back down.

Eh. Why not?

When my wolf had to go, she had to go.

As if she was aiming for it, the golden stream hit my ex's pillow, dead center. It pooled right into the fluffy fabric, soaking in. *Nice.*

Why shouldn't she mark her territory one last time? If I couldn't take them with me, Mike shouldn't get to use them, without this last reminder.

With my heart just a little freer, and my bladder a little lighter, my wolf hopped out of the bedroom window and straight into my new life.

CHAPTER 9
ROMAN

I had my hands elbow deep underneath the faucet—which I really shouldn't get into the habit of doing. It wasn't seen as "respectable behavior" from an alpha. But honestly, it took about three times as long to find a new decent plumber and schedule a time for them to come over as if it did for me to just fix the fucking leak on my own.

I'd already finished sorting out the problem. I could have just left it, but I wanted to make sure that I had everything fixed properly.

My beta, Nyx, cleared his throat to get my attention, but I didn't get up. I was almost—

"Your mate isn't with that boyfriend anymore."

Camille wasn't... what? My grip tightened on the faucet hard.

Oh, Fuck. Did I break it? Underneath my fingers were clear grooves where I'd dented metal. Damn. There goes all the time and money saved from not having to hire a plumber. I dropped the wrench and took in a calming breath so I wouldn't lose my shit. I stood to my full height, barely holding back the growl that threatened to rip its way out of my throat.

"What did he do?"

My hands were itching to make their way around his thin little neck. Going into another pack's territory to seek him out was an act of war, but my wolf didn't care. If he hurt her... I was going to redecorate that apartment with his viscera, paint the walls in his blood and pull him apart, piece by piece.

"We aren't sure how it happened. Yesterday, Camille was at the apartment. This morning, the boyfriend arrived holding hands with another woman."

"He dumped *her*?" That couldn't possibly be true. If it was, then Mike Bowman was an even bigger fool than I'd pinned him for. He had never deserved a woman like Camille. Never once been worthy of her. Then he went and turned around and threw her away like she was nothing? On second thought, I wasn't quite sure that I wouldn't be paying this Mike Bowman a visit.

"By the new woman's scent, it seems like she is pregnant."

If I'd still been under the cabinet, then the entire sink in the pack's main kitchen might need to be replaced. I clenched my fists as hard as I could as claws burst out of my fingertips, slicing into the meaty flesh of my own palms. I held myself very still. If I moved I wouldn't be able to stop. Not until I was at his door, breaking his face, just like I imagined every time I entered into the fighting ring.

Mike fucking Bowman.

I would never understand how a slimy little weasel like Mike Bowman managed to lure more than one woman into his bed. How *he* was the one who had the woman I'd been dreaming about. The woman I couldn't get out of my head.

I hadn't even been in her presence for more than a few minutes, and I had every curve of her gorgeous figure, her scent, that look in her eyes as they first locked on mine—all tattooed directly into my brain.

But Camille had turned her back on fate, ran from me without saying a single word... all for *him*. I couldn't quite make sense of it... that Mike Bowman had somehow gotten the love of the most devastatingly beautiful woman I'd ever seen, and then decided to knock up some other girl instead. That tiny runt of a man looked like he would break with the smallest twitch of my fingers.

"Wait..." I was so distracted by that asshole, I got my priorities all mixed up. "She was living with him. Where is she now?"

"Camille left the Evenfall Ridge territory..." Nyx's voice trailed off, as he shook his head.

That was a bold move, completely leaving her pack behind. But then again, considering how fragile her links were to her old pack, it wasn't really surprising that she would completely turn her back on them. It was risky. Her father was high-ranking and had enough standing that he could easily get his alpha's permission to track her down. If he wanted it, he could arrange a team to hunt her and bring her back, whether she wanted to be a part of their pack or not.

Well, he could try.

He wasn't going to get very far. If he showed even a hint of a plan to force Camille into any kind of situation she didn't want to be in, he was going to find himself at the end of my fists.

There was no fucking way that I was letting him anywhere near my mate.

"Did she approach any other shifters?" Nyx had to tell

me that she was at least making contact with a friend from another pack. Wolves weren't like the other shifters out there. We didn't function well in isolation. Besides what being alone could do to our psyche, it just wasn't safe out there. The more I'd gone over our records, the more I'd come to the same conclusion. We'd lost too many wolves. More than what could be explained away by the wars, or random bad luck. Wolf shifters were hard to kill, when we weren't killing one another. But there was something out there, picking us off.

"No. She's well beyond their territory, and hasn't made a move anywhere near other wolves."

"Where the hell is she?"

What was she planning? Wolf shifters couldn't survive on their own.

"We tracked her to a cave, in unclaimed land between the Stonevalley pack and our own. We couldn't get too close, but it seems that she is still in her wolf form."

Not that there was anything wrong with staying as a wolf long-term—her beast was as much of her as her human side. But it didn't seem like Camille had a plan.

Fucking *Mike Bowman* kicked my girl out of her home. If she got so much as a single *splinter* out there, spending her night in a cave, I was going to hold him personally responsible.

"Why don't you try to approach her again," Nyx asked cautiously.

I shook my head, as my stomach dropped with the memory of how the two of us sparked for the first time.

From the moment my eyes locked on hers, everything within me tilted— I was violently off balance as everything that defined me was fundamentally changed. Redefining me as much as the moment I shifted for the first time, becoming the wolf. There was nothing in my life that I wanted more than her, when I first saw the fire in her eyes. I could sense something fierce within her. Something that echoed somewhere deep in the lonely depths of my soul.

She clearly wasn't from one of the more traditional packs. Not the Edgerivers and definitely not one of the Stonevalley pack—those wolves were living straight in the past. No, my soulmate was wearing a leather outfit. Her outfit clung to a body that was luscious. She had full curves along her breasts and hips, and a toned athletic build. Thinking of her like that made me uncomfortably hard, and had irritation flooding through my veins... a slow current of anger that now seemed so much closer to the surface... *she was not fucking mine.*

Like a movie playing on repeat in my mind, I could see how her eyes widened, how she turned and *sprinted.* The sway of her long hair as it whipped around behind her. The harsh clacking of her heels that grew fainter as she ran out of the club... as if she was afraid that if she didn't get away from me fast enough that I would hunt her down and force her to be my mate.

Once she was gone, I was met with a sea of eyes staring at me. Every single shifter in that entire establishment was looking straight at me, then averting their gazes. None of them were doing it in the deferential way that paid respect to the alphas.

No.

They were looking away from the soulmark branded into my chest.

In one moment, I had become their worst fear.

I was rejected by my soulmate.

Not technically. My mate never said the words to completely dismantle our bond. She'd run away from me before even fully severing our ties. Just so desperate in her drive to get away. She'd never said the words, but this girl had rejected me, just the same.

Over the weeks, I'd considered seeking her out, just to shut down the bond completely. It went against everything I'd desired, everything I'd dreamed for myself... But I hadn't known how much longer I could keep my wolf restrained. Not when I could feel echoes of her pleasure through the bond. My mate was getting her needs met, and she didn't need me to do so.

Each time it happened, it was like a knife twisted beneath my skin. Digging in.

"She already made her decision." She'd told me no, months ago. I would stand by her decision, if it ripped me apart to do it. Camille had made her choice, and I would respect it. No matter how much my wolf was tearing me up from within. Frenzied, and at times desperate to seek her out. He didn't understand.

I would force myself to stay away, if that's what she needed.

Let this bond rip me apart. I could take it, even if it meant damning myself.

I would be damned anyway, if I let anything hurt her.

CHAPTER 10
CAMILLE

I woke up to my cellphone ringing angrily within my bag. My wolf cocked an ear at it. Growling, as if to say it would be nothing at all to rip through the fabric, find the noisy machine that dared to disturb her sleep and crunch it into oblivion in her jaws.

The threat to my cellphone was enough to rouse the human in me. *No.* I thought at my wolf, firmly. I could not deal with buying a new phone now, with my limited funds... even if I agreed that the sound was obnoxious. I recognized the ringtone. Hadn't bothered to change it, with everything going on. Mike.

What the fuck did he want?

He wasn't worth the transformation. I could just stay here as a wolf. The gods knew that I had neglected this form enough. I could use all the time I could get in my wolf form to make up for neglecting her.

But then again, I couldn't really just stay here as a wolf for the rest of my life. I was going to have to change back to my human at some point, might as well start now. It wasn't like I was pining after him or anything. I wasn't even the one texting him. *He* was texting *me*.

I pushed against my sleepy wolf, she growled once in her sleep, then gave over control of our body. The transformation wasn't any less painful the other way around. My bones lengthened, snapping in places, as fur was sucked back into my skin, as if my entire body was a mouth sucking in millions of tiny strands of spaghetti.

The first time I shifted, I stayed in bed for two days. It had been the most painful thing that I'd ever done in my entire life. Even considering all of the stupid stunts I'd pulled as a young and very dumb kid. But over time, I'd gotten used to the aftermath of shifting—how my skin was raw... the disorientating feeling in my core from all of my organs shifting around, and the splintering feeling around my bones.

It was cold in the cave. I hadn't really noticed when I'd been surrounded by my wolf pelt. The cold seemed to pierce all the way through me, deeper than my body. It was as if I was submerged in ice until the part of me that should be able to feel was fractured, leaving me numb.

I unzipped my bag and pulled my jacket over my naked form. It didn't really help. With a sigh, I dug through the bag, until I found my cell phone.

Did I really want to know?

Had I left something behind that Mike thought was important? Did my father suddenly remember that he'd knocked up my mother and was coming after his only offspring? Without giving myself time to think about it, I unlocked my phone.

Mike: Really?

Mike: Did you really have to take a piss on the mattress? What the hell is wrong with you?

Mike: Honestly, I thought you were better than that.

I was sleeping on a fucking cave floor, in the middle of a literal forest because this asshole had the audacity to break up with me on our anniversary. If there was something wrong here, it wasn't with me.

Did he expect me to respond? What a fucking waste of my time.

Mike should have known, seeing the way that I was around my father, you don't have to be dead to be dead to me.

His texts did not stop.

Mike: My mate is fucking crying. She's pregnant, she shouldn't have to deal with this. Why did you leave all of this shit behind?

Mike: What do you expect me to do with all this?

Mike: I swear to the gods, I will drop this stuff off at your fathers.

What was he expecting from me? Did he really think that all these texts were going to make me jump into action? That I'd feel awful for what I'd done, call him and make all of his problems go away? Was he expecting the old Camille, who thought that his raggedy ass was worth something? Who was stupid enough to love him. Shit...

Would the old Camille have dropped everything and bent over backwards for this loser?

What a stupid bitch.

I turned my phone completely off. I might need it for an emergency, and couldn't exactly charge my phone in a cave. Shit, I couldn't stay here. I kneeled on the cave floor, staring at the stone beneath me. Damn it, I was really hitting rock bottom right now.

I'd just gone out of the window and ran mindlessly, until I was out of the territory. Obviously that wasn't a long term solution. No matter how much I wanted to be alone, I couldn't just abandon other shifters. Lone wolves didn't survive for long. I knew that as well as any other shifter. But it didn't need to be for long.

Eventually, I needed to get into a new pack. That was going to take some careful consideration. Some of the wolf packs completely isolated themselves from all human interactions. They didn't even have cellphones for the gods' sake. If I wasn't careful, I'd wind up in the Stonevalley castle living like it was the Victorian era. They were sworn enemies to the Edgeriver pack. Honestly those wolves seemed a lot more normal, but I'd have to take a closer look. Maybe see if any of my old contacts were still willing to talk to me and let me know the full scoop. But there could also be a hidden drawback to joining their pack. I mean, besides potentially getting sucked into that war between the territories.

On the other hand, some of the packs out there might seem perfectly fine, and then you find out that your soulmate is in it.

What if I spoke to my soulmate... maybe we could—

Woah. Absolutely not. The wolfy part of my brain needed to back the fuck up. Maybe talking to my soulmate ended up with everything all hunky dory. Maybe he would be perfectly understanding about the fact that I had publicly humiliated him. Maybe he would be so bedazzled by my glorious smile that he would look past the fact that I had rejected him for another lover. Even assuming all of that... there was no guarantee that my mate would actually be a good fit for me. It was supposed to be fate. It was the blessing of the moon goddess and all of that. But one thing that everyone seemed to forget when dealing with soulmates was that she was matching your everyday shifters together. Maybe some of the shifters out there were epic heroes; valiant and noble and all that. But then there were the rest of us. If all the shifters had one true mate, that meant that even the assholes among us had soulmates.

At least that's what happened to my mother. Why should I trust the moon goddess to do any different for me? Why did I need to be tied to any man at all? After the whole incident with my ex, why did I even think for a moment that the solution to my problem was going to be found in another man?

This was all a lot to figure out, while sitting half-naked and cold in a cave. Just trying to figure out the entire direction that my life should go in, huddled here without any access to electricity.

You know what, fuck it. I didn't need to make all of these decisions now. I didn't need to decide which pack I'd have to eventually join up with to stop my wolf from going insane. I probably had years. Maybe even whole decades before I lost my sanity.

Why was I stressing myself out trying to figure out my exact plans for the rest of my life?

Twisting my neck to the side until it cracked, I stretched. Shaking my hands to get myself energized. Get the blood flowing, so the rest of me would get moving. It was time for me to stop sulking out in the middle of the forest in a cave.

Honestly, I'd been through worse than Mike.

I dug through my bag for a good pair of jeans; it was time for me to put my big girl pants on and figure this shit out.

CHAPTER II
CAMILLE

FOUR MONTHS LATER

The only soulmate I needed was my trusty rabbit vibrator.

Within me, my wolf growled softly.

She didn't approve of my noisy friend, my wolf twitched her nose at the scent of silicone.

Well, I'd take the smell of silicone over the scent of a typical shifter male. *They* smelled like betrayal. Like the synthetic floral stench of women's cheap perfume and cheating. Like the audacity to call *me* the other woman, after promising me forever.

But my new soulmate was perfect. Rabbit would never break my heart.

My new apartment was nowhere as big as my old place.

It didn't quite feel like home yet. Okay, honestly this place needed a team of four to five caring—but sassy—gay men with a building crew to be made into something that felt anything close to homey. It was a studio apartment that was essentially a glorified and overpriced chicken coop. I mean not literally. But it did have a smell of stale beans and smoke that seemed like it soaked into the wood. I knew for a fact that there was a slight infestation of six legged critters skittering about in the walls. It was enough to make me consider starting over... again. Or maybe just going back to that cave in the woods. I mean, I was technically homeless, but at least it smelled better. And there was no arguing with the cost of living in a cave.

For those weeks before I finally got accepted into a place of my own, I'd wake up in the morning completely in my fur. The first sweet rays of light would be hovering in the air. In that time before the rest of the world fully woke up, I'd take a morning run through the woods. There was something freeing about spending time in my wolf form. Before, it felt like I was simply letting her out to play, as if she was some kind of exotic pet that I had to maintain. But now, after having this time with her. Feeling paws pad through the forest floor, with the wind zipping through my coarse fur, running past all the smells in the forest and still managing to get a read on all of them—I'd never felt so alive.

I hadn't spent so much time in my wolf form in my entire life. It almost made the break up and subsequent isolation completely worth it. My wolf was more than some party trick, or some feral force within me that my human side had to keep a leash on. After spending time out here, experiencing her, living my life in her skin... it was clear to me that the wolf might be a different form, but that didn't make her different from me. My wolf was not other; she was another form of *myself*.

No, obviously I couldn't keep living in a cave. It was

impossible to keep all of my shit completely dry, and all of my electronics had gone dead in a matter of days.

But my new apartment wasn't all bad. It was mine, and no one from my past knew the address. Besides, I was totally adjusting to the break up. When I was wrapped up in enough fuzzy blankets, it almost felt like my heart hadn't been torn out of me and stomped on by everyone I thought I could trust. So there was that. The blankets were microfiber. Don't worry, I learned my lesson. They were thin enough that I'd definitely be able to pack them up and take them with me if things fell apart here.

After I'd finished with taking care of myself, I dragged my ass over to the scratched up vanity. It wasn't hard to do. This studio was small enough that if I turned on my bed I'd face the mirror in the dinky bathroom, that was more like a glorified closet. If I squinted and really focused, I didn't even need to leave the bed to get my makeup done.

With a sigh, I dragged myself up and over to the bathroom. Turning on the bare lightbulb vaguely made me feel like I was in a horror movie when it started flickering on and off. I had to time my eye-liner and lipstick application with the moments the light stayed on. I'd picked out a new shade that complemented my new hair color. After getting dumped, I did the stereotypical "new hair new me" thing and dyed it a vibrant purple. I'd never had my hair a different color before, but as soon as I saw my new look, I'd already felt more in tune with myself. I had to reapply to dye fairly often, as it faded drastically every time I shifted. But feeling more like myself for the first time in my life was totally worth it.

I thought that I would miss Mike, after spending five years together. But really, I think that I missed the sleek quartz countertops in my bathroom more. If I polished them enough, I could practically see my reflection on those countertops. Might even do a slightly better job doing my makeup that way, than in this scratchy mirror.

It was time for me to go to work amongst the humans.

THE BAR WAS QUIET TONIGHT. I'd already gotten a Pilsner and an English pale ale for some of my regulars. I scrubbed the countertops, though my nose was telling me that I was merely smearing the dirt around more than I was actually cleaning anything.

This job was easy. It was also less stressful on my wolf than working in the back of a department store or a shop; there wasn't as much going on. Less smells, less rattling noises. All things that my wolf would take as danger signs and would put her on edge for an entire shift. Even though I'd gotten my bartending license years ago, way back when I'd first come of age, I'd never actually used it. Mike had always said that it was too dangerous, or some shit like that.

The front door jingled and in walked a girl dressed for a date—sleek black dress with red lipstick. Shiny eye shadow that highlighted her doe-like eyes. Her gaze darted around the entire bar, then back to her phone screen as she bit the corner of her lipsticked-lip. She strode over to the bar, taking a stool and immediately opened her phone and. It looked like she was checking her messages. Every so often her gaze would dart over back to the door.

I placed a drink menu in front of her and then drifted away to give her space. I was making myself look busy by pretending to dry a mug that was already bone dry. The girl looked nervous enough about this date. I wasn't about to be the one to add to those nerves.

She looked over the menu for a moment, before meeting my gaze.

"What can I get for you?" I drifted back over to her.

"Is the watermelon wine any good?" Her voice was high and delicate like the high notes on a stringed instrument.

"Yeah, it's my favorite." I nodded.

"Can I get one?"

I nodded to her, grabbing a glass. I took the time to adorn the glass with citrus slices and a sugar rim, trying to make her drink look fancy. I thought that she could use a pretty drink. At least her pouty lips tugged up at the corners when she saw her cocktail.

For the next twenty five minutes or so, she sipped it slowly, between checking her phone and looking at the door. She sighed, deeply, and then started gathering her things together and rummaging through her purse as if she was about to pay off her tab. Dang, she just got stood up. She got dressed up so cute too...

The door to the bar opened once more and a man walked in. He was dressed alright, in well-fitted jeans and a button down shirt with the sleeves rolled up. He wasn't rushing or anything, just strolled right in, waving at her as if he wasn't almost half an hour late for their date. Or who knows? Maybe the girl was paranoid and got there super early, though it hadn't felt like that was the case. Anyway, my job was to get the drinks, not judge the dynamics of their relationship.

The guy smiled at her and it seemed like all was forgiven. Obviously, because women are stupid and men suck... aaaaand therapy just got higher on my list of priorities. As soon as I could afford it.

I went back to polishing mugs that did not need to be polished, in between taking the guy's drink order. He wanted a whisky on the rocks. I went back to being unobtrusive, trying to ignore them and failing miserably. Hey! There was nothing else to do. It was a slow night. Anyway, the guy was talking at the girl non-stop. From what I tried not to overhear, it was all stuff about himself. How he was going to be an influencer. How he was going to use the money and invest in stocks. Some tips he learned from his older brother, who was a life coach. He did not let her get a word in. But the girl didn't really seem to be upset. She was sipping her drink coyly and kind of batting her eyes at him.

What did she see in this guy? He was just some average human. My soulmate was ten times hotter than him.

Shit. Don't think about him.

Eventually, the girl began to fidget a little bit. She excused herself, then walked away in the direction of the bathroom. I was going to start inventorying the alcohol for the second time because I was bored, when I noticed her date gave a shifty look to the other guys at the bar. What the hell did this guy think he was doing? Then he huddled a little closer to her drink, taking a pill out of his inner pocket, cracking it open. He tipped the contents into her drink. My wolf senses picked up the sharp tang of barbiturates in this chemical cocktail. Oh hell no.

Are you fucking kidding me?

His date got back and the guy smiled at her, warmly. The picture of innocence, as inside I was fuming. I took deep measured breaths, trying to get myself under control before I screwed up and did something that would end the night with me in handcuffs, or packing up all my shit and finding another sleepy town to start over in.

As the girl reached for his glass, I plucked it out of her hands, glaring at the man. Putting all of the contempt I felt for him into my stare. I tightened my grip on the glass, shattering it, imagining that it was his throat I was holding.

The girl shrieked, looking at me horrified.

Oh shit. I hadn't meant to frighten her.

"This asshole was trying to roofy you." It was fine if this human girl left the bar terrified of me, but I wasn't about to let her go off without warning her about this guy. What if he tried something again?

The guy got all red as his face twisted up in anger.

"You're fucking lying!"

"Says the wannabe rapist." I scoffed.

He quickly scraped back his chair and stood up, puffing out his chest, as if I was the asshole who had just tried to date rape some poor unsuspecting girl. As if I could be intimidated by some wanna-be tough guy. He could get as mad as he wanted and it wasn't going to do anything to scare the wolf. Just like a mouse could get as annoyed as it wanted at the cat, but the anger of prey was never going to change the outcome of the fight.

"Call me that one more time. I fucking dare you." He sneered at me.

"Alright, that's enough Mr. rapist. You should get—" My words were cut off as the guy's fist swung straight at me.

Dude? What the hell.

Reflexively I caught his fist straight out of the air. I meant to squeeze it just a little bit, to kind of show to him that it wasn't nice to fuck around with people who were much much weaker. But then I heard the snap.

Whoops.

I swear, I didn't mean to break anything.

Even the strongest human male was no match for a shifter. The weakest of our kind could take him. And me? I was far from the weakest wolf shifter around.

There weren't many women who participated in the fight rings down at the clubs, but there were enough. I also knew enough about my own wolf's dominance and fighting instincts to know that if I had ever let myself fight in that ring, I'd be able to bring home a lot more serious cash. More than I'd gotten from busting my ass working down at the shop, anyway.

I guess I had my reasons. I can't even blame Mike for that one, a hundred percent. I'd needed to stay away from other shifters, but it was also always in the back of my mind that I needed to stay out of the spotlight. I couldn't have my father catching word of me. I didn't want to do anything that might catch his attention.

Now the man was shrieking like I had tried to murder him or something, trying and failing to pull his fist out of my grip.

Maybe I shouldn't make it so obvious that I was so much stronger than him.

I released his fist, trying to let go when he had stopped flailing, but he chose just that moment to wrench away hard. Since I had already let go, he went crashing backwards into the counter, smearing watermelon wine, bits of glass, and now his fresh blood over the floors I'd just mopped.

He clutched his mangled fist with his other hand dramatically, staring at me wide eyed. He was looking at me like I'd killed him, or at least like I'd crushed his hand. Which was a load of bullcrap. I definitely did not grab his hand hard enough to crush it—at least hadn't I thought I did.

The girl grabbed her purse and ran out of the bar. Hopefully she was running far away from the asshole who wanted to hurt her.

Now the human male was getting loud. Saying something about lawyers, about his connections and how he was going to get me fired and sent straight to jail. He shut up as I leaned closer, getting right into his personal space. At least on some level, even if he didn't know exactly what I was, he knew that I was something other, something *dangerous*.

"You can try to deny it, but you know what you fucking did."

His eyes widened and he slowly drew back, away from me. If only he knew how the wolf within me was debating right now whether this shit-stain of a person was worth the backlash if I went all out and just ripped his throat apart.

"I hope that you never run into me again. Because this?" I pointed to the little owie on his poor bitty fingers. "This is nothing." A little bit of the wolf came out, turning that last word into a snarl.

The man whimpered like a little bitch, but didn't say anything more to me. He gripped his injured hand tight like he was afraid that it was going to fall off, and marched towards the door. At one point he turned around like he was going to say something else. He got a good look at the blazing rage in my eyes, and thought better of it, exiting the bar instead.

I shook my hands, getting off drops of watermelon wine, glass shards and now the stench of asshole off my fingers.

"Damn," said Frank, a regular who came to the bar like

clockwork twenty minutes into my shift. He took another sip of his pilsner and went back to mucking about on his phone.

Not that I wished I hadn't helped that girl... I wouldn't be able to live with myself if I left someone innocent to their fate. But I had a feeling that this was going to come back and bite me.

CHAPTER 12
CAMILLE

I didn't get fired after I explained that the douchebag, Kevin Sawyer, had slipped drugs into his dates' drink, while she was in the washroom.

Kevin had sent my boss emails, complaining about me. My boss, to his credit, sent back the security footage that clearly showed Kevin tampering with a drink. I didn't hear anything else after that. However, after viewing the rest of the footage, clearly showing me shattering the glass and catching a punch single handed, my boss gave me the side eye. Though he didn't fire me, there was a coldness in our interactions that definitely wasn't there before; he viewed me differently now.

My life in this town wasn't anything special. The only reason I liked my current apartment any more than I liked living in a cave as a wolf was the fact that I had electricity. It wouldn't be hard for me to throw all of my stuff into a bag once more, and find some new place to live. There were bars everywhere, but I'm not going to deny that starting over somewhere completely new wasn't draining.

Just the thought of touring more run-down apartments,

putting down another security deposit, packing and unpacking all my belongings again... it was so tiring. Maybe I believed that after everything I'd just been through, the moon goddess owed me a break. And although I know that the goddess won't just make things go my way, I wouldn't mind if she cut me some slack for once. I felt like I had gone through enough shit already.

Should I have started over somewhere else? Probably. It would definitely be safer. Did I have the emotional bandwidth to deal with it, if I could possibly get away with staying in place?

No.

I launched myself into my work. I'm not sure exactly what I was trying to prove. Maybe if I was a hard enough worker, that my boss had made the right choice in not firing me? That I was the best choice, the most reliable person... when it came to arriving on time, inventorying alcohol and keeping the place mopped. As long as the occasional violent interaction with a customer wasn't an issue, I was probably the best employee on the payroll.

It was another slow day. After getting the usual drinks for my regulars, I already had the clipboard out. I was getting faster at the inventorying and paperwork. I knew what drinks my regulars liked to order, and what was likely to be running low. Even though I could tell the liquid levels at a glance from across the room, I made sure to go through all the proper measuring protocols. I picked up each bottle and used the tenthing method, recording each reading dutifully.

I heard the front door open, and greeted the new customers without looking—just one more bottle to measure and I was completely done.

My wolf was antsy, digging in her paws against my rib

cage as if she was scraping into the earth. As if she had to run. Halfway to tearing through my body and taking control of our skin.

What the hell had gotten into her?

I heard the high pitched burst of air, before I felt the prick. Automatically slapping my hand against my neck, and feeling the edge of metal.

What was that? What...

Before I could work out what was happening, my eyelids started getting heavier without me having any control.

In my blurred vision, I could see a pair of men stalking towards me. I tried to force myself awake. Even force my wolf to jolt free, bring on the change that would out me— reveal what I really am in front of all of these humans. I had no choice. I had to.

I clenched my fists tight, bracing for the moment that claws burst through my fingertips. Parting my lips for the howl I could feel within me, to burst out of my lips.

But it didn't come.

The woozy feeling in my brain was getting heavier, like someone was sitting on my mind. Forcing me to stay in place. And my wolf... my fiery and gorgeous silver wolf... I couldn't even feel her. It was like she wasn't there at all.

How? What the fuck did they?

My finger brushed against it, what must be a dart sticking out of my neck. I felt the burn against my finger-tips. *Silver.*

These men paralyzed the wolf within me with a single dart in my neck.

I watched in slow motion, like my brain was under water and this was happening to someone else. Forcing my heavy eyelids to stay open and watch as three men pulled zip ties out of their bags.

I sank to my knees even as I screamed at myself to stay up. I had to fight them. Had to. I was the only one who could protect myself. No one even knew I was here, and even if they did, I'd cut ties with my pack. Every family, friend, or... lover. All of them.

No, this couldn't...

I understood now. The silver? Darts? These men knew. They knew what I was. They knew that I wasn't a human, and they came equipped with exactly what they needed to take me down. *They came to hurt me.*

It was too late.

Darkness slid across my mind, carrying me over... to a place where I was all alone, and no one was coming for me.

CHAPTER 13
ROMAN

I was looking over paperwork in my office—holding my wolf back from shredding it apart. There had to be a better system than for alphas to have to approve all major documents. Yes, I was the strongest wolf in the pack. Yes, I had a strong protective instinct over all of the pack members... but reading over legal documents was not the same skill set as anticipating attacks and eviscerating enemies. There had to be alphas out there, that were otherwise amazing protectors and doing an absolute *shit* job of managing the finances. I felt like I was decent at this, but it took me forever—

My doorknob rattled for a moment and burst open. I was ready to snap at whoever disturbed me, I was going to have to mentally recalculate all of the totals for the third time, when I recognized my second-in-command.

"We can't find her." Nyx was breathless, panting hard. From his scent, he had sprinted. I could smell traces of pine and oakmoss from the trek across the forest. I must have been staring at him blankly, because he felt the need to elaborate. As if there would ever be any other *her* that got the adrenaline racing through my veins. As if anyone else could flip my world sideways and cause my heart to pound against my ribcage hard enough for me to wonder if it was trying to escape. "Camille, your mate. We have no idea where she is."

I swallowed down the fire in my wolf. He'd demanded retribution, and wanted to rake claws across my second-in-command for daring to lose sight of her. It was the one and only thing I needed. All I needed to keep my wolf in check was the daily report that my mate was safe. She might be living in a run-down apartment, isolated from others. But she was alive. Healthy and well. It was the only thing keeping me sane.

What the hell did that mean? She couldn't be gone.

"Tell me," I demanded, snarling the words until they were more wolf than man. Gritting my teeth to force the wolf jaws inside that threatened to burst out and sink into whoever dared let this happen.

"Camille wasn't at work. We even checked the inside of that bar and her scent had faded. She hadn't been there for hours."

It was her shift today. Over the past few months, I became intimately familiar with Camille's schedule. She arrived punctually, like clockwork, and stayed for an eight hour shift or sometimes longer. She wasn't the type to drop her responsibilities. Ever since she'd moved away, breaking ties with her ex-lover and her pack, she'd become something of a workaholic.

"We already checked her apartment, and all of her things were still there. Fresh milk was in her fridge. Bag left unpacked. Her scent trail leads from the apartment straight to work. From there, nothing."

This didn't sound like she made the choice to leave.

If she had run, there would have been signs of it. Nyx would have been able to follow her trail. Wolves didn't just vanish without a trace, as if they had never existed at all.

Camille was bonded to me. If something had happened to her... if she'd somehow gotten killed. Even the thought of it chilled me down to the bones, settled deep into my core, paralyzing me with cold. She couldn't be dead. I'd be able to feel it if she was dead.

Fuck. FUCK.

How the fuck had it come to this?

My mate... the other half of my fucking soul... and now she was just gone? And here I was, way too far from her, twiddling my fucking fingers. Just wondering what had happened to her. I'd failed to keep her safe. I hadn't even lifted a finger myself, relying on other wolves to protect her, when it should have been me the entire time.

Was she safe?

Since our bond sparked into being, I'd never said a word to her. Not after she'd made it clear that she wanted nothing to do with me. We might not have spoken, but I'd always had eyes on her. I'd pacified my wolf by silently keeping watch. Telling myself that it was enough.

But I knew better.

I knew. I fucking knew, that there was something strange going on with the numbers of shifters in the area. I knew that something wasn't adding up with our diminishing population. Even fucking knowing this, how could I have tested it? On my own mate? Imagining that she would be okay, that she would somehow be spared from this... just because I'd left a few guards to keep an eye out for her.

I'd been so fucking stupid when it came to her.

From the very first thought I'd had after sparking with

Camille, I'd had it all wrong. Since then, that same thought echoed throughout my mind, haunting me.

Fuck, I don't have time for a mate.

How could I have ever even thought that I'd been too busy for a mate? Like she was nothing but a chore on my list. I thought that her protection had been enough and just went on with my day to day tasks.

Why hadn't I at least gone to talk to her? I was acting like I'd already given up on my bond. I was acting like I didn't want her... when I craved her like an addiction. When it was a constant struggle to talk my wolf out of chasing her down. Why hadn't I just fucking done it?

Wolves weren't meant to live on their own.

I'd brushed her aside, as if her existence didn't matter at all. Maybe she was staying away from me because she believed that I was disgusted by her. That I was still angry that she had chosen another man over me at our first meeting. While I have to admit that my mate has questionable tastes in men... I understood her need to protect her boyfriend. Sometimes fate was unkind. Sometimes it was hard to bow down in the face of it. I couldn't fault Camille for making her own choice in the person she loved.

When I first met her, her heart wasn't free. Now that it was... how could I leave her to believe that I was indifferent? When I replayed that first moment I'd met her over and over in my head. Seeing her in my mind... those fiery violet eyes and her raw sex appeal. The luscious curves of her fit body were magnetizing, drawing me in. Again and again I relived those moments, just so I could be with her... even if it was only in my thoughts.

I was done pretending that I didn't want her.

Maybe she wouldn't feel the same... I could live with her choice if she didn't want to be with me. When she was single and had the opportunity to be with anyone, if she turned me down then that was simply my fate. I would accept it. I'd be forced to accept it. But then again, what if things were different now... how could I spend the rest of my life simply being okay with never even trying to find out?

Wolves had the potential to live long lives. Longer than humans. Some of us lived multiple human lifespans. How could I spend all of those years with myself, knowing that I had found my mate, and I chose never to even speak to her?

I closed the binder holding the paperwork at my desk shut. I was done pretending like I was alright with an arrangement where Camille's life was at risk. Where she was isolated.

It was time for me to go to her.

My human side was playing around with the idea that there was nothing wrong. Maybe my wolf was just overreacting again. What if she was taking a break, meeting up with a friend?

Sometimes the human side of me was an idiot.

If it turned out she was fine? And all that came of me visiting her was that she felt like I was disrespecting her wish to be alone... Well, fuck her wishes then. I was done pretending like I was okay with Camille blatantly putting herself in danger. I was going to do what I should have done from the start. It was time for me to seek her out. Find out for myself what was going on with her. If she didn't want my help, I'd hear it from her own lips.

Without warning I felt the crack, as something within my left shoulder shattered. Pain echoed through my arm.

What the... I grabbed my own limb, certain that I was about to find a bullet in it. But there was nothing. The bone didn't even seem to be broken. What the hell was...

A searing pain bit across my rib cage, burning me. I ripped off my shirt... to find that my torso was discolored. Silvery blue handprints formed on my shoulder and my rib cage right where I felt the pain. The colors within our soul-bond were pulsing with light. Pouring out from somewhere within the skin as if it had a life of its own. Like the flashing colors of a police car.

Whatever this was, this wasn't happening to me. My mate hadn't just wandered off, or quit her job. She'd been taken.

"She's being tortured." The words didn't seem like they were coming out of my own mouth. How could they? They were too calm. Much too rational for the realization that somewhere out there, someone was hurting my mate.

The ice in my heart settled over the human part of my mind, turning me completely numb.

"Assemble the fighters. All of them. Every warrior we have."

My wolf was licking his chops within me, anticipating the taste of blood that would soon be on his tongue.

Whoever did this, I was coming for them.

CHAPTER 14
CAMILLE

My entire face stung, constricted by the leather straps that lay heavy across both cheeks and held a wire basket over my mouth. It was so tight, I couldn't move without it digging into my skin, pinching and hurting me.

What? What is this?

I stared at the *thing* strapped over half my face, trying and failing to understand. My brain was static, refusing to process what I was seeing. The moment it clicked, the realization stung harder than the tight constriction of the straps. This was a muzzle.

The bastards strapped a wire cage over my mouth, one with the elongated snout—an *animal* muzzle, like the kind that you put on a snappy dog. It pinched at my skin because this vile contraption wasn't made to fit on me at all—it wasn't designed for a human head because who the *fuck* put muzzles on people?

They... didn't see me as a person. I was nothing but an experiment to them. An overgrown lab rat, waiting for them to experiment on... carefully tethered down and restricted so that I wouldn't bite. My eyes prickled with unshed tears that I refused to let fall.

I was powerless... could barely even move. They had me handcuffed to a cold gurney, in a small room with walls painted hospital-green. The only thing for me to see all night and day was the low light of the buzzing fluorescent lights in the ceiling above me. My sense of smell was muted by the strong chemical stench of bleach and disinfectant.

They had wedged a leather gag over my tongue, flooding my tastebuds with synthetic chemicals in the fake leather. The taste got mixed with the taste of my own blood. My skin started to tear in my fight to escape the pain, as I bit down, trying to grit my teeth.

But nothing I did was enough to escape it. Not with the bands of silver that these men had slapped against my wrists—they were thin. It had to be sterling, rather than pure silver. Enough of the metal to keep my wolf at bay, but not enough to kill me.

The silver slowed, but not completely stopped my shifter's ability to heal. My arm was still bent at an unnatural angle. A man wearing a white labcoat, with a more muscular build than the other men holding clipboards, had snapped my arm like a twig. My wrist was not only handcuffed into place, but the cuffs had thin silver wires piercing straight into my arm. Immobilizing the whole broken limb.

The rest of me *burned*.

My whole arm was on fire. Every part of me in contact with the silver was raw... inflamed. I clenched my one good fist against it, refusing to let them see me break. But it never stopped. Never let up. The searing throb of pain... as the silver pulsed through my arm like a high voltage bolt of electricity.

Worse than the pain... they cut me off from my wolf.

Exposure to silver... It was like the power of the moon intensified. It was much too close for my wolf. More power than either of us could process. My poor wolf. My powerful fighter... she was locked away somewhere deep within my body. Somewhere I couldn't reach her. It was like I wasn't a shifter at all anymore.

For the first time, I was totally alone. It felt as if I was ripped away from the fiercest part of myself. The part of me that could go feral, who would bite through my own limbs in order to escape. The one who wouldn't rest until these men were in shreds.

I'd had my family taken away from me... the man I'd thought was the love of my life. But this? Nothing hurt worse than having my wolf stripped from me. I had never been so defenseless. Alone. With nothing but my own spiraling thoughts to keep me company.

What the fuck were they doing to me?

What was going to happen to me? What were they doing to my arm, keeping it broken like this?

Alone, defenseless. There was nothing I could do, and I had no one but myself to blame.

There was no one coming for me.

CHAPTER 15
ROMAN

The transformation to wolf had never been so painfully slow. It was a fight for every claw that burst through each of my fingertips. I had to will every one of my bones into place as they cracked and my spine lengthened.

The moment I hit the ground on my four paws, I was ready to *run*. I didn't need to go to her job to pick up Camille's trail. My wolf knew exactly where to go. He could feel the bond, pulling us towards her.

I had seventeen wolves at my back, all of my fighters. Other packs had more soldiers, some were over a hundred strong. But my wolves were all dedicated warriors, fiercely loyal to me. I wouldn't trade a single one of them for dozens more.

Maybe it was because he had been denied, forced to ignore the pull to her for so long. Maybe it was because my wolf could feel her pain shuddering through his own limbs, but he had never run faster. My paws tore through the forest, and my pack struggled to match my pace, falling behind. I didn't slow down. The others would be able to follow my trail.

The bond guided me through a forest that ended abruptly at a clearing. I could pick up the scent of human dwellings, and further out, the suburbs. I didn't stop, or slow down. I couldn't stop. Not when I could feel the pain coursing through Camille's body as strongly as if it was my own.

Sidling up to a fence, I sprinted alongside it. Running through human territory was dangerous. I'd have to chart our path with care. Luckily, the path was near a dried out water drainage canal, a deep ditch alongside the main roads. All the cover we needed. Modern day humans tended to be distracted; on the phones, thinking about their to do lists. There was a small chance that they wouldn't even notice my pack. They also saw what they wanted to see. When my wolf ran fast enough, the average person would just assume that he was a large dog. Luckily with his dark fur, people wouldn't automatically realize exactly what he was. Most likely the humans would report a pack of wild dogs running through the drainage canal. The important thing was for us to move fast. By the time authorities came by to check out what was going on, we would be long gone.

I followed the drainage canal for over twenty miles before the pull from my bond showed me that Camille was in a different direction. I ran out of the ditch, utterly terrifying an older lady who was walking a small purse dog. I had to admire the neurotic bravery of the little guy as he pulled forward on his leash to challenge me. My wolf completely ignored him, as the lady scooped him up in her arms and started speed walking away.

The path led me straight to a run-down industrial area on

the outside of town. The buildings had faded signs and broken windows. The streets stank of piss and had clearly seen better days. I slunk down dark alleyways, padding around trash that seemed to have been left to rot for years. The only people around were clearly homeless, with glazed eyes that didn't even look at the large wolf running past them.

The trail ended at a rectangular building with boarded up windows that was somewhat isolated, on the outskirts. Despite the dirty exterior, clearly designed to make it look like just another abandoned building, this area was full of scent activity. Most of the smells were the trails of humans, coming and going through a reinforced steel door. But that wasn't the only living scent carted into this building. Though it was faint, I could sense a layer of beast enmeshed with human scents; it had to be shifters. There was the scent of the wild, of forests, and the distinct musky scent of wolf. There was an even fainter aroma. It was indirect, as if years old... or a scent that was caught on the clothing of workers passing through... was that bear?

But one thing my wolf was certain of, all of the scents of the shifters headed into this building, while not a single one had left.

Another smell in the air was calling to me—one that I would never forget. A scent that was carved straight into my being. As much of a part of me as any of my limbs, my beating heart. It was *hers*.

For the first time since the two of us touched in the shifter bar, and our bond lit across my skin, I caught the scent of my soulmate. It was acidic with fear and pain, but unmistakable. The sweetness of her floral shampoo... the delicate tang of her pheromones. She was here, within this building.

But how do I get to her? The entrance door looked like it

was made of reinforced metal with an industrial keypad lock. It wasn't anything that my wolf could manage with his claws or fangs. Luckily, my wolf trusted the strength of my human form.

Without hesitation, he slipped deep into the shadows and released his furs back to the human part of me. Once again, the transformation was sluggish, as I fought the echoing effects of whatever these assholes were doing to my mate. Letting my bones rearrange and realign, snapping back into human form, as fur pulled back into my body, leaving me completely bare.

Whatever was happening here, this was bigger than just Camille. Though she hadn't intended to do it, my mate led me straight to the mystery I'd been trying to dig up for years. I knew this had something to do with whatever was happening with the number of shifters dwindling in our territories.

The rage that had flooded through my system for the past few months was calm now, hyperfocused on just this moment. I cracked my neck, loosening a bit of strain leftover from my transformation. Within me, my wolf licked his chops in anticipation.

These humans might have thought that they'd covered their tracks well. From the looks of things, they'd been getting away with taking and hurting our kind for years. Whether they knew it or not, they were dead men walking... from the moment they put their hands on the shifter that was never theirs to touch.

Any hair out of place, any scratch on her fair skin these humans would repay a thousand times. From the pain echoing in my own limbs, something told me that I would be decorating these walls with their viscera and blood.

CHAPTER 16
ROMAN

Alarms blared from the moment I busted down their armored door. I ignored the noise of it, as I maneuvered through the maze of rooms. I felt her location through the bond, drawing me toward her stronger than any magnet. But the layout of this building was designed to frustrate me.

Guards pulled their rifles on me, but hesitated at the sight of a naked man striding towards them, splattered in blood and holding the decapitated head of one of their scientists.

I hadn't been able to hold myself back, when I smelled her on him, under his fingernails. This was one of the men who had hurt her. At least the man was proving useful in death. Some of the high tech rooms required a retinal scan to get through.

What I'd seen already had hardened my hearts against the rest of the humans working here. None of these men were innocent. They must have known what goes on behind these walls, and still they continued to work here. They'd chosen wrong.

The guards pulled themselves together enough to aim their rifles, and I smelled the heated metal tang of silver from within the barrels of their rifles.

Not today, humans.

I hurled the scientist's head high over the guards, and one of them actually panicked, aiming away from me to fire at it. He blasted the head into pieces that splattered everywhere. As shards of skull and brain matter ricocheted around the room, I *moved*. While the guards were shielding themselves from the gore, I launched at them. Claws erupted through my fingertips, slashing sharply across the thin flesh of one man's throat. I kicked out, sweeping my leg in an arch, knocking over one guard into another, following him down with a series of blows until my fists were red with the remnants of his face.

A blast in my shoulder diverted my attention. A gaping hole revealed where the bullet went clean through. I couldn't even feel any residual burning from the silver bullet. Or maybe I didn't feel the pain of it, because I couldn't. Not with the rage still coursing through me in a steady beat. Hot enough to burn the rest of me away, until there was nothing left but this haze of all consuming anger.

Controlling me as completely as if I was nothing but a puppet on a string—a puppet with a bottomless urge to kill.

Something in my expression must have tipped the last guard off, because he backed away from me until he was against the wall with nowhere to go. He actually dropped the rifle to the ground, holding his hands up in surrender.

"No, please," his voice was a needy whine, a fly buzzing in my ear. "I—I'll give you anything..."

I'd grabbed his throat hard, cutting off the rest of his useless whining. With just a bit more pressure something in his neck cracked. I let him fall, his body crumpled awkwardly on the floor, before realizing that maybe he might have been able to point me in the direction of my mate.

It didn't matter. No use crying over spilled humans. Not when the bond was pulling me harder than ever towards her. She was so close. So *fucking* close.

I fished around in a pile of human goo with the consistency ranging somewhere between tuna and jello. I gingerly pulled out a blue eyeball from the mess. Excellent, this was much more portable than carrying an entire human head.

The next door, marked simply with an H6, had to be opened with another scanner. The first try the scanner beeped and flashed red. I wiped the eye off on my torso, clearing off some of the debris and tried again. This time the scanner flashed green, and the lock disengaged with a loud click.

As soon as I opened the door, I could tell that she was not in this room. The two rooms I'd opened before both held shifters who'd looked more dead than alive. Both male wolves, both unconscious. Though I hated leaving them, the sight of what had been done to them made the panic crystalize in my veins—I was so tense with nerves it was surprising that I hadn't shattered apart already.

Like the others, this room wasn't empty... but this prisoner was awake. In the back corner of the cage, a burly man sat on the floor. Even through the harsh stench of silver, it was obvious that he was a shifter. Though his scent was faint, the silver had cut him off from his beast for too long, this man wasn't one of the wolves.

He cocked his head at me, regarding me silently. His eyes, though shadowed so dark they looked bruised, were clearly the eyes of a predator.

The need to get to Camille was pounding at the back of my mind… but I was also working with no information. What if this shifter knew about where they were holding her? What if he could give me some information on what they were doing here? Walking in totally blind was a recipe for disaster.

"How did humans get their hands on you?" I walked closer to the bars surrounding this shifter on all four sides. Close enough that I could feel the heat from the silver threatening to burn away my skin. Crossing half the room helped me place his scent; he was a bear shifter. I'd never spoken to one before. Bears were by nature, more solitary than wolves. Even when they stopped by the shifter clubs, the bears always seemed guarded, like they were merely passing through. But bears were built like tanks, and wary as all hell. It was hard to imagine a scrawny human taking him out.

The man snorted like he was disgusted at himself.

"Tranquilizers and handcuffs made from silver alloy." His voice was rough. Raspy like he was no longer in the habit of using it.

Tranquilizers and silver handcuffs were nothing but modern day poisons and traps. The human had to resort to slimy tricks to trap our kind. But the real question was *why*.

"What's happening here?"

"They're experimenting on us… to understand our fast healing, and long lifespan. Trying to harvest it for themselves."

The humans would never be able to imitate our healing capabilities, any better than they would be able to go outside and bottle up the moonlight, or the blessings of our goddess herself. Humans like to think of themselves as the masters of the earth, but there are things that they would never understand.

"How long have you been here?" I eyed the spiderwebs growing in the corners of the cage, the old dirt that seemed to have seeped into the corners, giving this room a neglected look.

"Haven't been able to track time... But it was twenty-nineteen when they caught me, and put me in here."

I shook my head. They never should have been able to imprison a proud shifter for even a single day. "I'm sorry, brother. That was five years ago."

"That long..." He looked off into the distance, as his whole body stiffened. "I'd just found my mate."

The pain in his voice stirred something that was frozen and numb deep within my own chest. Something that recognized the yearning for the other half of one's soul; a feeling like a part of my own self had been cut away and stolen from me... a part that I could never get back, because it was my own heart ripped away even as a cheap imitation of it was still beating within me.

I held the eyeball up to the scanner on his cage, adjusting the position until it beeped. After a moment I heard the click as the lock disengaged. I slammed the cage open with my claw tips, ignoring the sharp burn of the silver, opening the door wide. "Go to her, then."

The man rose to his feet, bending his head to avoid the metal frame. Though he wasn't much taller than me, his presence seemed to crowd outwards once he was out of the cage, making the room feel much smaller.

The bear shifter was twisting the manacles around his wrists, eyeing them speculatively. A ring of blackened skin, dead and peeling, formed around his wrists from the constant contact with the toxic metal. He gripped the manacles firmly and pulled, hard, in a white knuckle grip. Tugging until something snapped in his wrist and the poison metal pulled straight off. He dropped the band, letting it clatter to the ground.

The freed hand was limp and useless, and his other hand was still shackled. He rolled his wrist, staring at the metal band as if it was a puzzle he'd spent too long trying to piece together.

Silently, I reached out, extending my hand. He stared at my hand for a moment, a bit like I might stare at a venomous snake, before holding his hand out to me. I gripped the silver, ignoring the burn that hissed across my palm charring my skin and pulled. Yanking hard, even as the bones in his hands cracked and something in his shoulder popped. Not stopping until the metal dropped to the ground.

"What's your name?" Nothing changed in his voice or expression, now that he was freed. But white hot anger was seeping out of his pores, until the small room was flooded with the heat of his wraith. That bone deep need for vengeance.

It was a need that I recognized. Having one's mate ripped away, when there was nothing I could do about it... it went against everything that I was. In my center, in my core, I was made to protect my mate. Being separated from her went against more than biology. More than the wishes of the Goddess herself; it went against everything that I am.

"Roman Volkov, alpha of the Blackwood wolf pack."

"Roman Volkov," the shifter stated through gritted teeth, the sound coming out deep and gravely, as he began to transform in front of me. His bones creaked as they realigned, snapping into place, as the bear rose to the surface. "I owe you a debt."

Once fully transformed, he let out a feral roar and charged out of the room that was his prison cell. He was an enraged, nine-hundred pound grizzly, rampaging down the halls, looking like he was out for blood.

Behind me, a series of wolves howled. My pack had finally caught up with me. From the utter fury in their call, they were as ready as I was to tear this place to shreds.

Despite the terror for my mate driving me forward, and the rage boiling my blood, my lips tugged upward.

CHAPTER 17
ROMAN

The palms of my hands were blackened, but that didn't stop me. It barely slowed me down, as I tore the metal off every cage door I could find. Ripping through the cages was helping to soothe the ever present roar in my blood—the need to tear and mangle the ones who had hurt my soulmate.

The humans who'd run this facility were taken care of far too quickly. We'd long since decimated their active guards, and taken down the teams of scientists on duty. There were still humans hiding in places throughout the facility—I could smell them, and the rancid stink of their fear. But they weren't mine to deal with. The enraged roar of a bear or lone snarls, followed by shrill human screaming, reverberated down the concrete hallways. As much as the need for revenge needled at me, like ants biting from beneath my skin, constantly itching at me to just do something. Fight them. Kill them, for what they had done... this wasn't my fight. Not when she still needed me.

Behind me, after I rushed through a room, my wolves would check over the victims. One of my beta wolves had pulled a set of keys from a body. Like the rest of the metals in this hellscape, it was laced with silver. My pack handled the keys gingerly, passing it around to one another taking turns holding it, and unlocking all of the handcuffs that they could find.

All of the shifters that we were releasing now were wolves. There were no other bear shifters, and honestly I was surprised that they were able to catch one in the first place. Even among the shifters, bears rarely went to public events. The one I'd found was just incredibly unlucky.

Most of the wolves that were released were males, from various packs. Some of them were in awful shape. The prolonged exposure to silver had rotted them out from the inside. Those ones, we pulled off all the silver we could see and then had to move on. At that point, it was up to them to fight. To call on their wolf and ignite the transformation.

From some of them I heard the snaps of bones, the familiar yips and groans of pain, the squelching of muscles pulling and reshaping. Enough for me to know that not all of the freed wolves had lost their fight. Once they were able to transform into the beast, their bodies would be reborn, erasing almost all signs of the physical damage done, besides the deepest scarring from the silver that no amount of shifting would ever be able to remove.

But others… even after pulling the silver off of them, the shifters didn't move. Out of the corner of my eyes, I watched as the handcuffs were pulled off a man. The only sign that he made that he was freed was one long and drawn out sigh. Acting like he was readying himself… so still that it was as if he was already dead. Each wolf I saw in that state pulled at me, had me checking my bond, feeling the connection.

Camille.

She had to make it. From the first moment I'd looked in her eyes, I could tell that my girl was fierce. There was no way that she would give up. She couldn't. Not now. Not when I was so close.

Under my breath I whispered every promise I could think of to the goddess. That I would never again let Camille out of my sight. That I would protect her to my last breath. All I needed was for her to be okay.

She had to be alright... *Please, let her be alright.*

I saw the flash out of the corner of my eyes, of a brilliant blue that burst out all at once, illuminating the gloom with its bioluminescence.

My eyes locked on the source of it, just behind me, where my second in command had taken a turn at breaking the shifters out of their handcuffs. His hand was still making contact with the wrist of a shifter; she was pale, and far too skinny. Even from here, I could see the indentation of her ribs through her shirt. Though she looked young, her hair had all blanched to the cold white of a much older person. But her face was dainty, with petite features and a button nose that made her look just like a doll.

Her eyes opened, fixed on the light burning across her skin, as it permanently marked the exact point of contact on her skin where she had touched her soulmate for the first time. Light spread from her wrist, in a series of constellations and lunar phases, leaving behind a mark with one exact match. Revealing to her that the wolf who had rescued her was her soulmate.

Nyx tore his eyes away from the bright flash of light erupting across his skin, and met my gaze. An unsaid question hung in the air as he looked at me. I nodded once, understanding what he needed immediately.

Yes. See to her. Care for your mate, pull her out of this hell hole.

I felt the same devastation within me. How was he supposed to do anything else? Watch over the rest of these wolves with the full knowledge that the woman whose soul was a match for mine was in pain? Being so close and not doing anything was torture... so close. Completely defenseless and surrounded by the worst kind of humans. Humans filled with greed and a history of hurting our kind.

Nyx wasted no time scooping his mate into his arms. Carrying her cuddled close against his chest, as he gazed over her worriedly, looking over every one of the marks against her skin. Taking in her too skinny form.

Nyx's new mate whispered in a raspy voice, that I could hear clearly, even as Nyx carried her further away, holding her like she was the most precious being in the entire world. "My name is Willow."

Marked by the constellations of their soulbond, showing that they belonged together, she gazed at Nyx with stars in her eyes.

I felt a twinge somewhere deep in my chest. Pressure beating where my heart was supposed to be. *Would Camille ever look at me, like that?*

No. Shut up. Shut the fuck up.

She was out there, in pain. I was her damn mate, I couldn't waste time thinking about the way that she would look at me, when she was surrounded by dying shifters.

This was a life and death situation and I wouldn't let myself get distracted by something as useless, as utterly *human* as jealousy.

I had to find her.

She was close. I could feel it.

CHAPTER 18
ROMAN

I abandoned the rescue attempt of the other wolves, running straight for Camille like I'd wanted to do from the moment I'd felt her pain burst across my arms... if I was being honest with myself, it was even longer. I'd wanted to go to her for fucking months.

I broke down doors, ignoring the human scientists that shrieked and soiled themselves at the sight of me, only pausing long enough to take note of their scents. If our paths ever crossed again, I'd remember these men.

Their deaths weren't as important as her survival. I didn't have time for revenge.

But I burned the memory of what they'd done to her in my brain, deep. Somewhere I'd never be able to forget. Where that knowledge could wait for the chance... then I'd come back for them.

These hallways were maze-like, and arranged with no particular order. There were combinations of letters and numbers on the doorways, and if the doctors in charge had put them into an order, I couldn't make heads or tails of it.

As soon as the retinal scan registered in a room labeled F4, and the door cracked an inch open, I knew.

There she was.

Her scent slammed into me, and her sweet fragrance—coated in the acid bite of cortisol and the sharp stink of silver—had my wolf frenzied within my chest.

I hadn't been this close to her since the moment that our bond sparked into life. I could picture the exact moment perfectly, as if her image was burned beneath my eyelids and tattooed right under my skull. Those plush lips. The heat in her high cheek bones as she'd blushed. Her features were so pretty and dainty, she looked like a doll or a pixie pulled straight out of a story. So lovely.

For that brief moment, when euphoria rushed through my veins, when she was each and every one of my fantasies come to life... before she ran from me. I remembered just as clearly, that her lovely eyes widened, taking me in. Not in surprise, but in horror. How she'd bolted like she'd been afraid of me.

But now... if it wasn't for her scent, or the pull that felt like it came from the middle of my chest, drawing me toward her, I might not even be able to recognize her from that memory.

Now she was way too still.

Camille was covered with thin wires, piercing into her skin. Each and every one of those thin wires burned—I could tell by the fire mirrored on my own skin. The bond let me feel her pain, echoed on my own body, though without the damage. It was enough to push away her wolf, stripping her from her beast until she was as defenseless as a human.

Her eyes were clenched tight with tear streaks staining her cheeks. She'd bitten her lips so sharply that there were deep gashes with blood staining her chin. Her arm was broken in at least two places, and these sadists masquerading as scientists had pierced her mangled limb with thin strands of silver. Her hands—even the broken fucking ones—were handcuffed to a metal gurney, and the skin around each wrist was dead and ink-black. *Why? What the fuck were they doing? What the fuck was the point?*

Hanging up on a hook on a wall, was a heavy muzzle, one of the heavy duty ones with wire baskets and leather straps. The thing was drenched in the scent of Camille's blood, and the chemical cocktail of her pain.

They'd muzzled her. They put a fucking *muzzle* on my mate.

Camille was so disoriented, she'd made no sign that she even noticed that I was here. That anyone had come into the room with her.

Seeing her like this made me see red. My blood pounded through my veins. I needed to hunt them down. Every last one of them. Commit to memory the humans I'd passed by on my search to save her... I instantly regretted every single human that I'd killed on the way over to her.

I'd done it all much too slowly.

I wanted to draw it out so they could feel it. Pull them apart inch by inch. Slice them open from their neck to navel and do it nice and slow. Let them watch, powerless to do anything to stop it when I etched out justice on their fragile human bodies.

They fucking *dared.*

They put their dirty and worthless little human hands on someone who was not theirs to touch. Only the fact that she was still in pain in front of me, stopped me from turning around to each of the humans I could find and smashing their worthless hands. Grinding them down until they were as useless as mud and dust. Stop them from ever being able to hurt anything ever again, before tearing them slowly. Slow enough to watch them... close enough to watch all of the light leak out of their eyes at their end.

Fucking Focus. She's in pain, dumbass.

I tugged gently at the wire connected to her skin, ignoring the burn of silver against my fingertips like putting my hand into an open flame, as I carefully drew it out and away from her. There was a mild bit of resistance, like pulling out a long splinter, but I was able to pull the wires out of her—so many fucking wires. Drawing them all out of her as gently as I could.

They'd already put her through so much pain. I wasn't going to be the one to put her through anything more.

As the last of the silver left her skin, Camille began to stir. Whimpering softly, as she moved her arm.

She stiffened, as she realized she wasn't alone, and hazily forced herself awake. Her eyes kept on glazing over, unfocusing as they tried to find me.

As her gaze met mine and her sweet violet eyes locked on me, this time in recognition—I made up my fucking mind.

I didn't care what she'd done. Camille was coming with me. I didn't care if pulling rank made her hate me. She wasn't going back to her isolated job, miles away from my protection. Nor was she going to step foot back in her tiny apartment.

I would never let her get hurt again.

CHAPTER 19
CAMILLE

The unrelenting fire coursing through my broken arm slowly started to die down.

What?

I wasn't stupid enough to believe that the humans were showing me any mercy. I had to get up. Brace myself for whatever they were going to do to me next.

It took me a moment to force myself awake, after I'd braced against pain for hours. But those eyes. Those steely green eyes, the exact same hue as the blur of wildness as I ran through the forest... now staring at me with enough heat, I should be in flames all over again.

It was him.

My soulmate... how was he here?

Oh, shit.

As I got a closer look at him, I noticed that he was completely naked.

He was covered in blood—human blood. I recognized the scent of that man in the lab coat who had broken my arm.

But that meant... Did he kill that human? *For me?*

Did he come here to save me?

But why would he? *No one had ever saved me before.*

Even Mike. Back when things were good, yes he had "saved" me from having to live with my crazy father. He had "saved" me from loneliness and isolation, but would he have put himself in any danger? Could I imagine him fighting through and killing hordes of humans to come rescue me?

No.

Not even when things between us were good. Definitely not for a girl who had turned him down. If Mike had to face a fraction of the rejection that I'd put my soulmate through, he wouldn't have lifted a finger for me.

Something fragile, deep within me began to crack. I thought that every last spark of love for Mike had already died. I didn't realize that some dregs of affection for him remained until now. They'd been brutally extinguished. I guess some sad little delusional part of me was stupidly holding out for affection wherever it could.

My soulmate stepped closer to me, and I swallowed, as my throat went bone dry.

I thought I'd imagined what he was like. Maybe it was because I hadn't stood quite so close to him. Or it might have been because I'd been blinded by the panic of the moment. But I don't think that I'd ever been so close to a wolf who was *this* dominant.

I was handcuffed to the gurney, and the constant sting of the metal against my wrist was cutting me off from my wolf, but even without her, I could sense it as easily as any other physical trait. Power radiated off his form.

My soulmate's gaze shifted to the handcuffs, holding my broken arm in place. He gripped the metal, careful not to jostle my arm. His biceps flexed as he pulled at the metal loop, both of his hands gripping it hard—even though I knew that it had to be burning the inside of his palms, like reaching into an open flame, my soulmate didn't hesitate.

After a moment, the cuffs bent, before snapping all at once.

Oh. *Damn.*

Silver was a poison to us. It corroded our skin, and ripped our wolves away. After enduring the blistering pain of it, I'd forgotten that it was a soft metal. He quickly pulled the snapped edges of the band further apart then dropped them, letting them clatter on the floor. Without stopping he wrapped his hands around the other band. All of his tendons stood out as he strained against the metal, his arms shaking faintly, until the second cuff broke apart.

He freed me.

My soulmate cursed, looking at the raw and blistered edges of my wrist, where the traces of silver had made direct contact. His fingertips hovered over my wounds, tracing a line over my injuries, before he drew his hand away without touching me.

"Can you shift?" His voice was deeper than I'd expected. Low and gravely and full of concern.

I shook my head.

Now, even with all traces of silver gone, I couldn't reach her. My wolf was still sleeping somewhere deep inside of me. Which was a pity. If she could see him this close again, I bet that she would be wagging her tail frantically, like an overeager puppy. She'd been pining after her mate for months.

He looked me over, carefully like he was committing every inch of me to memory, his gaze lingering on each place where I was injured—my broken arm and the open sores on my wrists. My entire body felt ragged, like I'd taken a savage beating. After bracing against the burns of silver for who knows how long, all the energy was sapped out of me.

Gingerly, with my good arm, I pushed myself upright, painfully slow. Though my wolf was asleep, the predator in me fought to hide my weakness, fought to move the muscles that had already been punished and tortured for longer than I could stand—I lost control, almost falling back on the cold gurney, when a strong arm caught me.

In one smooth motion, he wrapped his arm around my back, as his other hand went beneath my knees, lifting me like I weighed nothing. He leaned close to the shell of my ear, and said in his low voice, "I'm going to get you out of here."

He stalked out of my cell, holding me steady. Carefully. Cradling me against him like I was the most precious thing in the world. I wasn't sure if it was the relief of getting out of there and away from the pain that had almost shattered me... or if it was the warmth of being held, but I couldn't remember a time when I'd felt so safe.

Which didn't even make any sense. I barely even knew the guy. I didn't even know his name. This was only the second time I was meeting him, and he was splattered in blood. *But in the blood of the people who'd hurt me.* My wolf would be swooning if she was here to see this.

I was unconscious when I'd been carted into this facility, but there was no way the labs were meant to look like this.

The hallways were a bloodbath.

Broken glass and smashed lab equipment littered the floors. Bodies lay mauled next to claw marks so deep that grooves were carved out of wood and concrete. Something sticky hung from the light fixtures that looked suspiciously like they used to be organs.

I didn't have the energy to think about the gore around me. I relaxed into my soulmate's arms, as I idly watched the trail of destruction rush by. The rocking motion of his steady footsteps were lulling me half to sleep.

After fighting against the pain for so long, all I wanted to do was—

"Don't go back to sleep." The words were jarring—not said in a hostile way, but infused with enough of an alpha command that I was powerless to resist.

I let out a soft groan that sounded like a whine, as my eyes snapped back open.

"Some of the shifters who fell back asleep after we freed them aren't waking back up. I don't know if they will ever wake back up." My soulmate shook his head. "Silver sickness."

I'd never heard of that before. But the way that disgust colored his tone was more than enough to tell me everything that I needed to know. There were other shifters he'd tried to save here, besides me. It sounded like going to sleep after having the silver removed could be a death sentence.

Honestly, I wasn't fully coherent. If I wasn't so out of it, I probably wouldn't be laying in this man's arms, docile as a newborn pup. The exact same man I'd run from. The one who had me looking over my shoulder, anxious that I was being followed. For months. But I had enough fight left in me not to give up. Not now, as I was being rescued.

I forced my eyes to stay half lidded, forcing back the darkness, as the darkness called to me.

CHAPTER 20
ROMAN

My mate cradled in my arms, felt like a ticking time bomb.

Once I would have been thrilled just to have her so close to me. I had forgotten her sultry appeal. Her rosy lips. Sweet curves on her athletic build. She had a wild feminine charm that dug its claws deep into my brain, ensnaring me tighter than any trap. Holding her, with her skin and that sweet scent pressed directly against me, was driving my wolf absolutely feral. He was agitated, prowling close to the surface, just beneath my skin, growling within my chest.

She had opened her eyes, and was struggling to stay awake after I freed her from the silver. I'd seen too many of the wolves I'd freed stay still. Their bodies lay in an odd in-between place, hovering in the gray area between life and death. Failing to come back to life after their ordeal, but their powerful shifter bodies were refusing to let them die.

Camille was far too pale. I moved her slightly, to press my hand against the corner of her wrist, and felt the desperate beating of her pulse. Her fingertips were shaking faintly.

Fuck.

My mate was going into shock.

I held her tighter and moved as fast as I could, without jostling her as I caught up to the rest of my pack. They were still moving as a unit, seamlessly, breaking the shifters out of cages and removing their handcuffs. Nyx, my second-in-command, had already taken his mate to safety, so I turned to the next wolf in the hierarchy. Rain snapped to attention the moment I walked into the room, nodding her head deferentially, awaiting my commands.

"We'll have less than an hour before this place is swarming with cops. Free every wolf that you can find. Tell them that any wolf found here will find protection in the Blackwood pack."

"What about the ones who can't wake?" Rain's gaze flicked over to the unconscious shifter she had just freed. Though he was no longer handcuffed, the man lay still on the gurney as if he was already dead.

"Do what you can for them, but don't get caught." I looked down to my soulmate, who struggled to stay awake. Her breaths were far too shallow. She honestly looked like she was ready to pass out again. Seeing her like this... I'd never wanted vengeance more. "Kill every last human you find here."

I left my generals behind, as Rain huddled around my fighters and began to rapidly delegate orders. I had to get my mate out, far from the humans who found out today what happens to those who fuck around with nature.

Holding her as close as I dared, tight enough to keep her from jostling her broken arm, I ran. Fast. Until the hallways were a blur of chaos, and until we were out of the facility and through the door that I'd broken in what seemed like a lifetime ago. Fast enough that the homeless men on the street weren't quick enough to look up and see a naked and bloody man pass by. Non-shifters were really triggered by nudity, but I couldn't waste time to go track down some clothes. I had to keep moving, and get the hell out of here. Get away from all of these wandering eyes. Had to get my mate to safety.

I didn't stop until the pavement beneath my bare feet gave way to soft earth, and the run-down industrial buildings gave way to residential housing and finally—*finally*—the crisp pine and musty damp of the forest. The trees and foliage were dense enough that no one would be able to follow us easily. Technically, this was borderlands, in between the territories carefully protected by wolves. While the ordinary people might feel at home surrounded by their concrete and machines, for shifters the forest was home. I'd be able to protect her here.

I panted, catching my breath. I hadn't even really paid attention to my surroundings, after giving completely over to my all-encompassing need to move. To get her to safety. Towards the end of my mad dash, Camille started feeling heavier in my arms, as she began to roll in and out of consciousness.

She had been forced from her wolf for too long. If she was able to reconnect with the beast inside of her, it should be able to accelerate her healing. She didn't even need to fully shift. If she could just call back to her wolf, from wherever dark pits this ordeal had pushed that part of her, that would be enough.

"Come on, fight it." I put a hint of authority into my voice. Normally, I hated using the alpha command on unconsenting wolves—but not now. Not when my mate was slipping away. Even after I had stolen her back and carried her into the safety of the forest. After I killed the people who'd hurt her... freed her. I'd fought off more than just the humans, I had fought against fate and my own stubborn idiocy.

I couldn't lose her now. I'd do anything. Anything, to take away her pain. If I could reach in and take it on myself, I would. If I had to kill dozens more. Anything. I'd do it. If she would just snap out of it—but she didn't respond to the command at all.

"No, sweetheart," I shook her, wincing as the motion rattled her broken arm.

Camille whimpered, burrowing her head closer into my chest. Her eyes sprang open, and she held them open for a moment, before they started to drift once again to half mast. It was as if she was fighting against a force as irresistible as gravity. It was an inevitability.

Fuck. I was losing her.

What the fuck was I supposed to do now?

If she fell unconscious now, would she ever wake again? Had the silver poisoned her too severely? Had I come for her too late. I'd promised her that I wouldn't ever let her get hurt again. Had I already failed her?

No. I couldn't lose her. Not now. Not when she was safe. Not when I'd finally gotten my head on straight, after pulling it out of my stubborn ass. I couldn't lose her now, after everything. I dropped to my knees and whispered every promise under my breath to the moon goddess. To fate. To anyone who would fucking listen. I couldn't lose her.

Was this my punishment? For my first moment of weakness, when I thought I didn't have time for her. I didn't know what I was thinking. I must have been out of my mind to think even for a fraction of a moment that I didn't want her. I would never question the plans of the goddess again. I would be a stronger alpha. Anything.

Just, *please*.

Camille let out a long sigh, and her body went limp in my arms as her eyes started to roll back.

"No. Camille, no." I held her tighter to me. Pressing my forehead against hers, as if that would be enough to press some of my own determination into her. My arms started to shake, as pressure crushed the inside of my chest, as if my heart and lungs were squashed tight into the space of a pinprick. My blood roared in my veins, uselessly primed to get me moving, to do something, to fight this.

I grabbed her cheeks and slammed my lips against hers. The kiss I gave her was brutal. It was a collision as electrifying as the first touch that sparked the soulbond between us. I pushed through her plush lips, deepening the kiss. Hard. Until the tang of iron was on my tongue from where I split my lip against her teeth.

I don't know how long I pressed my mouth against her still lips; it could have been a stolen fraction of a moment, or a vibrant connection that I could be lost in for eternity. But then, Camille's lips moved as well, kissing me back. Slowly. Passionately. Every brush of her lips against mine was intoxicating. She nipped my bottom lip, sending a bolt of lightning surging down the full length of my spine. I pushed against her harder, losing myself in the rush. Needing to feel more of her.

Camille's violet eyes snapped open, staring at me wide-eyed, like she was staring at a predator. She broke off the kiss with a harsh gasp. Confusion lined each of her features, even as her scent changed subtly. The soft feminine fragrance was joined by the earthy musk of the forest as her wolf returned to her. She swallowed, nervously and leaned away from me.

Fine, let her hate me. Let this kiss be the first and the last moment of contact I ever got with my mate. I would accept her hatred gladly.

As long as she was alive, I could take it.

CHAPTER 21
CAMILLE

My wolf flowed into me. I could feel the beast in my pores, back in the core of me. Hovering right under my human form, living right under that first thin layer of skin. She was there walking across my rib cage, wagging her tail from within my body. Excited to finally, finally spend time with the mate who'd saved her.

Mate, mate, mate.

I could practically hear the word in each one of her growls and yips, like a chorus of howls playing on a loop in my mind. My wolf was bounding within me, practically vibrating in pure glee. Things were simple for her: Mate had found her. Mate was a good protector. She'd known it from the moment she had first seen him that he was good, and would take care of us.

His gaze was so heated, it felt as if my body should be inflamed all over again. He was looking into my eyes, like I was precious. The expression on his face looked like he had been absolutely devastated and I was the answer to all of his prayers.

I didn't even know his name.

He'd saved me. Somewhere deep in my bones I knew that I would have died in that old run-down laboratory if he hadn't saved me. He'd killed the human who'd broken my arm—I could smell that man's scent on the blood my mate wore.

But that didn't even make any sense. I'd rejected him, in front of hundreds of other shifters. I'd publicly humiliated him... I thought that he'd be angry at me for the rest of his life. That's just what high-level alphas were like. My own father could barely be bothered with me, because I had the nerve, the utter audacity, to be born a girl.

When shifters first found their soulmates, everything was supposed to fall into place. At least that's what everyone said. Hearing about bonding from other shifters, it was like the heavens parted and the goddess would sing a song so sweetly that all the stars would burn brighter, announcing the perfectness of one's fated match. Watching my own parents, I'd never believed that in the slightest.

There was no guarantee with soulmates. No matter how devoted my mother was, her soulmate had never treated her right. Mother had always blindly believed in the will of the goddess. She'd blame herself before waking up and admitting that my father treated her like trash. I promised myself that it wasn't ever going to happen to me.

I'd assumed that if I didn't fall over at his feet, that my soulmate would just forget about me. That we would go our separate ways. I hadn't even really thought about him after Mike had unceremoniously dumped me.

But then... kissing him felt so damn *good*.

I pulled away from him... I didn't even know him! All the while, I ignored the little voice in my head whispering that I was making a mistake. *Do it again... make him mine.*

Why had the most intense sexual experience in my entire life have to be with my mate? It was only a damn *kiss*, and somehow it felt better than sex. The touch of that man's tongue was like pressing against a live wire, lighting up every single switch on my body for sex.

It didn't help that he was naked, and I could see all of him. I didn't even need my wolf to see how power radiated off of him. All of his muscular body. Every inch of him was *fine.* Especially a certain part of him that was standing at attention, and very large.

Goddess, that would feel amazing.

This was stupid. I had to get control of myself before he smelled my arousal. I couldn't let myself get so drunk off one kiss that my brain completely rotted and I turned right into my mother. I wasn't stupid enough to put myself in a position where I let a man take advantage of me.

But he'd just saved me... He'd risked his life for me. Killed those men, all for me.

When had anyone ever done that for me before? What if he wasn't like the other alphas? He was already showing me through his actions that he wasn't anything like the dominant men who'd made my life hell. Maybe—and this was a big maybe—he actually wasn't a stereotypical alpha asshole. Maybe he deserved a chance? At the very least, I should thank him for saving my life.

"You came for me," my voice was breathless and airy, like someone I didn't even recognize. "I don't even know your name."

It was as if my words startled him out of a trance. His gaze on me focused, as if he was in the middle of a hunt and one wrong move was going to lose him his prey.

He had placed me down on some soft moss, with one arm still wrapped around my shoulder, supporting my weight. His grip on me tightened, slightly, as if he didn't want to let me go.

"I'm Roman Volkov, alpha of the Blackwood pack."

Roman. Now I had a name to go along with the face that had been burned into my memory, just as it was burned into patterns on my skin. I liked the way that it flowed on my tongue.

There. I asked him for his name, and the world didn't come apart. There wasn't a seismic shift within me, making me more tightly bonded. I could have asked him for his name long ago.

I took a deep breath. Time to be brave.

"Thank you. I thought I was going to die there." I admitted quietly.

Apparently, it was the wrong thing to say. Roman shook his head as if he was disgusted.

"It never should have fucking happened. It was my responsibility to take care of you, and I failed." His voice was low and gravely. The muscles in his neck corded, with anger so hot I could *feel* it.

Why the hell was he blaming himself? None of this was his fault. He wasn't the one stupid enough to get captured and kidnapped. How was he even supposed to protect me when I had isolated myself from other wolves? From him?

"I ran from you."

"That never mattered. I had you followed, I could have found you. I could have chased after you myself. I fucking didn't, and because I didn't, you got hurt. You almost died."

I shook my head slowly. There was too much to unpack. He'd had me followed? For how long? Did that mean he could have come after me at any time? But I'd been watching my back for months, and I'd barely suspected a thing...

"How is it your fault that I almost got killed?" If I was feeling better, I would have rolled my eyes.

"Because you're mine!" He snapped.

Oh, shit. I could feel it the moment that all the feminism left my body—evaporating out of my pores, and leaving me a mushy mess. Some idiotic part of me wanted to just lie down, expose my belly and say yes alpha.

I do not find possessive assholes sexy.

At least, I shouldn't find possessive assholes sexy.

Damn it.

"I knew that you were putting yourself at risk, and I. Did. Nothing." Roman snarled each word until it sounded more like an angry wolf than a man. "I could feel it. Everything that they did to you. I remember every bit of your pain."

Roman gritted his teeth and closed his eyes as if he was trying to force himself to get it together. "You are coming with me." His expression was hard and left no room for argument. "I will never let anyone hurt you ever again."

Within me my wolf perked up, wagging her tail like a puppy. She knew that he was perfect for her, that he was going to protect her. Well damn, was I going to let my mate and my wolf decide for me?

Why wasn't I protesting against this?

Did I even want to go back to my roach-infested apartment? Could I even go back to my job? The job where someone had managed to drug me, and steal me away to experiment on me? I was probably fired anyway.

He took a deep breath as if he was trying to calm himself down, and looked away from me.

"Even if we aren't together, I am not going to let you put yourself in danger." His angry tone dissolved into bitterness.

Something in me deflated at his harsh words. Roman wanted to take me with him, but he still didn't want to be with me.

Right. We weren't together. We wouldn't be together, because I had publicly rejected him.

I did it all for Mike.

Because I am the world's biggest idiot.

CHAPTER 22
ROMAN

I might have fucked up everything with my soulmate even more than I'd already fucked things up with her. Camille hadn't said a word since I told her that she was coming with me. She was a strong woman with a fierce streak of independence, and I wouldn't be surprised if she tried to run the moment I put her down.

As soon as we passed through the borderlands, some of my tension eased. We'd traveled closer than I'd like to the Stonevalley territory—close enough to scent their patrols. The Blackwood pack had maintained a truce with the Stonevalley wolves over the centuries, but I didn't want to give them the shadow of an excuse to pull us into their never-ending wars.

The forest darkened from the very first steps into my territory. Thick tree trunks and large overhanging branches twisted upwards, blocking out the light. We were cloaked in the bittersweet, almost spicy scent of old-growth woods. It was as if time had been eaten away, and we had been plunged from midday into twilight.

Camille leaned closer into me, though I wasn't sure if

she was aware that she was doing it. I felt every touch of her soft hands reaching against my bare chest as she held onto me, instinctually.

For the first time since my soulbond sparked into place, my wolf wasn't agitated. Every breath I took, he used to luxuriate in Camille's scent. He had it memorized to the point where I'd be able to find her in my sleep. He still thought I was an idiot for waiting so long, and for once I wasn't arguing with him.

Buildings emerged suddenly in a clearing in the forest, dissipating the gloom. Most of the communal structures were made of clay bricks filled with a rich earthy scent; the dining hall and kitchen were built large enough to accommodate a pack more than double our numbers. Though she wouldn't be able to see it from the outside, the renovations were nearly completed. For the past couple months, I'd hired trustworthy contractors and learned the skills myself when no one was available.

Through the dense leaves, I caught glimpses of the pack houses. They were scattered about in the forest to give each wolf privacy. Would Camille feel more comfortable in one of the refurbished pack houses? I immediately dismissed the idea. That was too much like abandoning her again. No. Until I knew that she was perfectly safe, I was keeping her close.

The pack was unusually quiet for this time of day. There should be some of the pups running around and causing a ruckus. The pack's gamma wolves would normally be out and about, working on the cooking or the laundry. Instead there was barely anyone outside.

The scents of the rest of my pack were behind closed doors, lingering behind the curtains. With most of the fighters still back at the human facility, the remaining wolves were shutting in and staying safe.

Nolan, an older beta, respectfully nodded to me, but otherwise hurried about his business. He knocked on Nana Rose's door. When she answered, her eyes flicked my way, lowering in deference before she let Nolan through, shutting the door behind her.

If either of them thought it was odd that their alpha was carrying an unknown female shifter who had clearly been injured, neither of them said a word.

I brought Camille to my house, placing her down with care in the guest bedroom. I'd finished this room long enough ago that my presence in it wasn't overpowering. The rest of the house was heavy with my scent and pheromones. In this room, the bedframe was made of sandalwood, encasing everything in the buttery scent of the sweet wood. It was exactly the kind of relaxing environment she would need to recover.

One hopeful part of me wondered what she thought of the place. I'd discussed the plans with the contractor and had overseen a lot of the repairs myself. Every choice I'd made, from the wood detailing, to the trim, the neutral color pallet and the modern organic aesthetic—it had all been designed to make a comfortable space for both the wolf and human within me.

I squashed that thought violently. Obviously she wasn't going to be thinking about design choices after she'd been tortured and then rescued by a man she barely knew.

It might have been too late from the very start between the two of us. The timing of when we'd met—it was all wrong. Maybe if our bond had sparked between us before she'd met that fucking asswipe, Mike Bowman, or after he'd revealed that he was cheating on her, maybe then I'd have had a chance with her. Maybe if I'd had it in me to give Camille some space after her ordeal, then we would be able to work things out between us. But the thought of letting Camille go out back to her isolated life, far from my protection, far from even the basic support of any other shifters... it had me baring my teeth, and ready to kill.

There was no chance in hell.

I'd rather live out the rest of my life alone, knowing that she was alive than put her at even the smallest amount of risk.

I knew that I was acting like an asshole. Ripping her choices away would never result in the two of us being able to connect and have a real relationship. Maybe I wasn't built to be with someone. Relationships seemed too expensive for my taste; if the price was her safety, it was too high.

"That door leads to the bathroom," I pointed it out, struck by the sudden need to get away, before I ended up causing any more damage. "I can go get you a change of clothes."

My hand was at the door, ready to get out of the room and give my soulmate some space, when her scent changed, suddenly spiking with the sour scent of anxiety. I turned, frowning to see what she needed.

"Can you stay with me?" Camille turned beet-red as soon as the words were out of her mouth. Her jaw hung open as if she was trying to figure out a way to take back what she'd just said.

Oh, hell no. Immediately, I turned back. I wasn't giving her time to second guess herself.

CHAPTER 23
CAMILLE

What the hell had I just gotten myself into? Why had I asked him to come back?

The most powerful alpha I'd ever seen was now stalking closer to me. His gaze was hot and heavy on mine—because I'd asked him to. Nothing would be able to hide the hunger that he had in his gaze. He stared at me longingly, as if he'd gone without for his entire life, and now here I was, laying before him like the finest cut of mouth watering ribeye.

Blood was mostly dried across his sculpted body. Far from being disgusted by it, I couldn't look away from how the reddish hue clung to each hard ridge of his sculpted body, adding to the muscular definition.

That absolutely ravenous look that Roman wasn't quite able to hide... maybe it meant that I had gotten this all wrong. He wasn't even angry at *me*.

I mean, I could tell that he was angry that I'd isolated myself and put myself at risk. The fact that I had gotten hurt, that someone had actually taken me away, that had made him downright savage. He had seethed all over with rage, until I could feel it crackling in the air all around him —but none of his anger was directed at me. He didn't look angry at me at *all*.

I'd had people angry *at me* enough times in my life that I could tell the difference; it was something I'd grown up with. I'd only had to duck out of the way of razor sharp claws and fangs once, before I'd made it a habit to monitor my dad's moods. When powerful shifters were angry, they were lethal. The only reason I had survived this long was because I had honed my ability to read emotions down to a science.

Before I'd managed to get out, I'd been a convenient scapegoat for all my father's misplaced ire, and I thought that it made me an expert on the anger of dominant wolves. They did not forgive. My entire childhood was spent walking on eggshells around the alphas and high-ranking betas, and I'd learned the hard way that the only thing to do was submit or get out of their way. Angry dominant wolves would accept no compromises. No apologies. I'd written off Roman, assuming that he would never forgive me for running from him. I thought that he'd hated me, and that was the end of it.

I'd done nothing that a mate was supposed to do. I hadn't even given him the shadow of a chance. I'd given him *nothing*. But when I needed him, Roman came and saved my life.

He wasn't looking at me with disgust, or like I was someone to be ashamed of. I could smell the heavy spice of his pheromones, hanging over the room like fog, coating everything around us with the heavy scent of his desire—or maybe it was my desire that I smelled in the air.

He was looking at me like he wanted to fuck me.

It had been so long. I wasn't even talking about just sex. How long had it been since my ex had even touched me like he'd wanted *me*? Or was I just a convenient outlet that he could use to get himself off? When was the last time I was touched by someone who cared? How long had I just let myself be used?

The way that Roman was looking at me right now was like he craved me. Like his entire body was on fire and I was the only thing that could soothe the ache. Like *I* was his addiction.

Roman was a sleek line of solid muscles. Every inch of him was rock hard strength that I was itching to touch. His body was stained in the blood of all the people he'd killed for me. He steadily stalked closer and closer to me. Was there something wrong with me for thinking that was fucking hot?

His eyes were half shut, drowning in the haze of pheromones and lust that were flooding into this small room, his and mine both. Whatever he had meant to say to me was lost, as he reached out to my cheek and tipped my chin until my eyes met his. Until I was lost in his forest green gaze, as lost as if I'd started a mad sprint into the heart of the wilderness.

"If you keep looking at me like that, I'm not going to be able to stop myself." He stroked his thumb lightly against my cheek, holding me as if I was precious, but oh, so fragile. He held me like he was afraid that if he let go, I was going to break apart.

I didn't know anything about this man. A few hours ago, I didn't even know his name, and had never even spoken to him. What I wanted to do to him flew in the face of every rule I'd ever made for myself to survive the high-ranking alphas.

I didn't know him, but something within me came alive under the touch of his hands.

My near brush with death made me want to chase after that spark—the connection that burned between us. Touching him made every single cell in my body ignite like I was caught against a live-wire.

More than I was afraid of dying, I was afraid that I would never again feel the way it felt when his lips burned against mine, like he was breathing life back into me. Going back to my life without him would be like going through the motions—living like a corpse.

I don't know exactly why, but I felt like the reason and logic had flown up high, and gotten lost in the web of delicious pheromones and lust.

He was right here, and his touch felt better than sin, and he was looking at me like he wanted to devour me whole.

I wanted him to sink his teeth into me.

I was lying to myself when I said that I didn't know him. The deepest, wildest part of me knew him. From the very first moment I looked into his eyes and saw an echo, a reverberation, the other half of my own soul. That part of me knew, more than it knew anything else, all the way down to my bones, that this man would *never* hurt me.

You can do this. Be brave.

I leaned closer into his space, watching his pupils bloom with desire, and gently brushed my lips against his in a soft kiss.

"Maybe I don't want you to stop," I murmured against his plush mouth.

It was as if I had unleashed a tsunami wave.

Suddenly, Roman was on me, his lips pressing hard against mine. His tongue traced against the seam of my mouth until I tilted my head and allowed him in. He deepened the kiss, wasting no time tangling and wrapping our tongues together. I felt each touch and slide echoed deep in my core. My clit throbbed for him, as every inch of me heated under his touch.

He bore his weight down on me as he plundered deeper into my mouth. The change in friction as his tongue slid against mine—soft, then harsh strokes—felt unbelievably good.

So fucking good. Too good, and at the same time not enough. I was a tense bundle of want, practically vibrating with tension, and my salvation was so close. I needed him to give it to me.

He was so hot, every inch where my skin touched his bare chest felt like I'd been lit on fire.

I'd let this man do anything to me. I didn't even care that it was fucking crazy. I was too lost in the feel of him, how his touch lit me up from the inside. How in my entire life, I had never felt more alive than right now.

I've wasted so much time.

I just want a taste of him.

"Tell me you want this." His words were a snarl, more animal than man. His eyes were fierce, as if his wolf rising to the surface, was demanding to make his claim on me.

"Roman," I moaned his name, until it sounded like a plea, a benediction.

I didn't just want this—I needed it. Needed him so badly my body was vibrating. Every inch of me was so sensitive and desperately empty. The thin layer of my clothing separating me from him was worse than any torture.

I wasn't going to survive another moment if I didn't get to experience the feeling of my mate's cock inside of me.

"Fuck me."

He didn't make me beg. Didn't make me ask twice.

Immediately he grasped the thin cotton of my shirt, tearing it apart, ripping it until it lay in thin shreds across my torso. Roman's claws burst through his fingertips and sliced through the lace fabric at the front of my bra, wrenching it apart with one quick jerk. My pants and underwear quickly followed, as he tugged them down past my ankles, leaving me completely bare to him.

Roman grabbed my left wrist, the one that hadn't gotten injured, and slammed it down on the bed, holding me in place, as he pressed harder against me, climbing onto me. His free hand ran down the curves of my breast, in a light trail across my belly and over my hips.

Every inch of me he touched was burning, consumed with pleasure. Roman traced a scorching path of desire down my body, and I needed him. Closer.

Roman was right there with me, his touches turning rough with need. He squeezed my hip hard, before tugging my thighs apart and settling in-between.

Then I felt him, blunt and thick, as he slid the head of his cock against my pussy. He held himself back, using his cock to brush against my entrance without sliding inside. Back and forth he teased me with what I needed. Each stroke against me was electric, jolting me with pleasure every time the head of his cock brushed against my clit.

I was so wet for him that I felt my arousal drip onto the bedsheets.

Roman had sparked a fire within me, consuming me. His weight on top of me... his rough touch on the curve of my breasts, just inches away from my nipples... the delicious friction as he slid his hardness against me, taking me right to the edge until I would do anything for that little push. For him to press deeper... just a little bit more. He was already there, so close to being inside me.

He felt so damn good. So perfect.

The pleasure coiled within me, tighter and tighter—until I burst. My vision whited out in an intense flash of light, as the tension within me spiraled apart as I came. Waves of bliss pulsed from my core, spreading out to each of my limbs, washing away all the stress left in my body until I felt like I could melt straight into the mattress.

As I lay there, whimpering with the aftershocks of the most intense orgasm of my life, Roman adjusted his cock, sliding it down until it was notched just inside of me. He gently cupped his palm against my cheek, staring into my eyes like he was trying to memorize them.

Biting my lip, I nodded.

Yes. I knew exactly what I wanted—him.

Roman thrust hard, in one brutal stroke, filling me to the hilt.

My head flew back against the pillow, back arching as I moaned.

Fuuuck.

He was so *big.*

Roman ground his hips against mine insistently, pressing his cock so deep I'd never be able to forget his exact shape, his thick girth against my walls—what it felt like to take every inch of him.

"Roman!"

His name on my lips was a moan, a desperate cry—for what I didn't know. The weight of him over me, inside of me, it was too much and yet not enough.

Roman swallowed my moans in a heated kiss, taking

my mouth as fiercely as he'd taken my pussy. Letting me know with each possessive touch that my body was *his*.

Then the harsh press of his mouth against mine softened to something gentle, something sweet. He was kissing me like a lover—like he loved me.

He broke off the kiss, whispering into the shell of my ear, "are you okay?"

I bit my lip. His cock was so huge, it was just on the border of too much, as the pleasure veered off into something painful. But I held on to that sense of trust I felt for him, instinctually. A part of me refused to believe that he would ever hurt me. Roman would take care of me.

"I can take it." I whispered.

He gave me one more sweet kiss, before burrowing his face into the crook of my shoulder, and he began to *move*.

He slammed his hips into mine. Rhythmically. Pounding into my pussy. Hard.

I gasped, and dug my nails into his back, needing something to hold on to. If I let go, surely I'd break apart.

I'd never been fucked like this before.

Each thrust was savage, rocking through my entire body. Jolting me so powerfully, I felt it reverberate all the way down to my toes. He was like fucking a force of nature. Fucking a whole stampede of wild animals. A storm rather than a man.

He fucked me so deep that he was in my bloodstream, swimming through my veins, driving himself straight into the core of me. Fucking me so that I could feel it, deeper than my bones, that our connection went beyond our bodies. We were bonded by our very souls.

Everything I was, the essence of me—he was the same. With every raw and powerful stroke of his strong body, he was making sure that I'd never forget.

He caressed me, feeling along my breasts. His fingertips curved over my nipples, stroking them in his possessive grasp until they hardened into peaks. He felt along my waist and the curve of my hips, touching me like he wanted to memorize every inch of my skin.

When his lips met mine, it felt like he was worshiping me with his mouth, pouring all of his desire into me, all of his longing for me.

I'd never felt... so wanted.

I'd been vulnerable, naked in front of others before... but never before had I felt so seen.

One sharp thrust intensified all of the tension within me, coiling it until I was shaking with it. Until all the pleasure was too much, rising to a fever pitch.

I shattered—bursting into pieces as I came.

My walls fluttered, contracting with wave after wave of pure bliss. Every inch of my body was sated, lulled into contentment, as the most complete sense of satisfaction I'd ever experienced washed over me.

Roman clenched my hip hard, as his eyes darkened, drinking in the sight of me coming down from my climax. With the deep guttural growl of a beast, he pulled almost entirely out of me and slammed back in. Hard. Like a man possessed. Again and again, over and over.

He pounded into me, fucking me mercilessly as he chased after his own release.

I wrapped my legs around the small of his back—all I could do was struggle to hold on.

His grip tightened against my wrist, hard enough to bruise, and then his whole body shuddered as he came. Roman moaned deeply—with a sound that was primal and intensely masculine. My lower belly quivered in response.

I could feel him pulsing deep within me in thick spurts.

I'd never done anything so reckless, so wild and impulsive as to take the soulmate I barely knew to bed. Even if I found out later that it was a mistake, that I'd given him power over me that I wasn't willing to give—I didn't even care.

I'd do it all over again in a heartbeat.

CHAPTER 24
ROMAN

Fuck. I had completely lost control.

I had meant for our first time together to mean something. I wanted to give her so much pleasure that she would never again question that we were meant to be together.

But the moment that she told me she wanted me, I lost my damn mind, rutting into her like I was nothing but a damn animal. What the *fuck* was I thinking?

I woke up with my mate curled up against me, her hand resting on my chest. A part of me never wanted to be separated from her, even for a moment—wanted to luxuriate for a little longer in this connection. There was no way that it was going to last. As soon as she woke up, she was going to be pissed at me.

I was still covered in blood—blood of men who'd put their filthy human hands on my mate. I'd have to burn these sheets later. There was no getting the stench of dead men out of Egyptian cotton.

Though I hated to do it, I slipped away from my mate, moving slowly enough not to jostle and wake her. Camille didn't stir; I'd thoroughly worn her out. It was a sign that I had absolutely no self control. At least, not when it came to her.

I took the opportunity to finally shower, and found chunks of—was that viscera in my hair? I'd taken my soulmate for the first time while covered in small fragments of organs?

Goddess, *damn it* all.

I found my cell phone completely dead and fiddled around the living room, looking for the charger. I left my phone to charge, stalking over to the kitchen to fill up the coffee pot. I had to make it so dark that it might as well be injecting coffee grounds directly into my veins for it to have any impact, before my shifter blood burned the caffeine out of my system. But after my colossal fuck up last night, I needed all the help I could get.

Last night was...

I wasn't one of those shifters who'd saved myself for my soulmate. My wolf was too fiery for that. Making my rounds on the fighting circuit was barely enough to placate him. But with my ranking, any shifter who I ended up taking to bed could lead to disaster. It might be as simple as bestowing favor and rank on an unworthy bloodline—even that could have repercussions for generations. But in the worst-case scenario, if I slept with a wolf who ended up as the soulmate to a high-ranking alpha in another pack, it could lead to warfare.

I grew up watching the blood feud between the Stonevalley and the Edgeriver wolves, enough to know that I had to do everything in my power to make sure that I would *never* subject my pack to that kind of violence.

Over the years, whenever my beast became too agitated, I took humans to bed. They were always one night stands. No strings attached. Though obviously I'd made my wolf wait too long since the last one. When was the brunette... was that really three *years* ago?

I'd thought that I'd held back as much as possible, but most of the time I scared the living shit out of humans. It didn't matter how much I tried to prepare them. Even when I thought I was being gentle, or that I was going slow, I always managed to freak them out. Before I even got close to coming, I could scent it in the air, how their desire had melted away into the acidic scent of apprehension and fear.

I left more than one human in tears.

That was when I was trying my damndest to go gently. With Camille, I had lost my shit before the first moment I sank into her. I lost control at the look of her hooded eyes on mine. I lost control when she even *hinted* that she wanted me.

Hope that you enjoyed it. That was the last you're ever going to get from your mate. I thought to my wolf bitterly. But he just scoffed at me, like *I* was the one who was being ridiculous.

With the taste of tar-like coffee on my tongue, I turned my phone back on to find fourteen missed calls and fifty-nine new text messages. I winced as I used my thumbprint to unlock it.

Right.

We had been in the middle of a potentially lethal mission, where my fighters were up against armed and dangerous humans. Something else that I had completely forgotten while I was blinded by pussy, and making a complete ass out of myself.

I opened my phone, bracing myself for the worst, as I scrolled down to the first voicemail left by Rain.

"Alpha, I got a status update for you..." there was a

sound in the background of harsh banging that could have been gunfire, or metal being ground and ripped to shreds. "We hot-wired a van, and loaded the unconscious shifters in. Ran into a bit of resistance, the human experimenters had some military-grade backup. We're under fire, trying to—"

The call broke off abruptly with loud gunshots and Rain's cursing.

Shit.

For all I knew, my fighters could be dead right now, or captured by the humans.

My wolves were *my* responsibility, and I hadn't even been there. I hadn't even *known*.

I wanted to give the silver-sick wolves a chance—Goddess knows that we couldn't afford to lose more wolves. But I would have *never* allowed my pack to risk their lives when I wasn't there for them.

I went through more of the texts with my heart pounding, every limb ready to bolt into action. Fuck, I had essentially abandoned my wolves when they needed me...

Even when I read the message that they had managed to give the humans the slip—with some hair-brained scheme that broke multiple traffic laws—the adrenaline coursing through my veins refused to slow. I wasn't sure if I wanted to rip Rain a new one, or reward her for a job well done.

Her next messages made the need for revenge itch beneath my skin.

Rain: Three of the unconscious shifters
stopped breathing on the drive.

Rain: The others aren't looking good. Some of them were shot. Should I take them to River territory?

Was she downplaying the damage that my wolves had taken over the mission? I should have been there. Even if we hadn't lost any of our pack, they brushed too close to death for comfort.

But they'd lost *three* wolves? Already?

Even during the shifter wars, it could take *years* to take down one of the dominant shifters. Losing three during transit was catastrophic.

We were already struggling with our population. Some shifters took *centuries* to conceive. It was part of our extended lifespans. The transformation into wolf form acted as a hard reset on our bodies, shifting us back to the moment where we were at our physical peak. For our women, it could delay or put a halt to ovulation. Before the Stonevalley alpha's heir had his son, there were no new births among the local shifter packs for at least a decade.

Goddess, what if that had been Camille in that van, and she was one of the shifters who'd died?

I shut down that thought immediately, before my wolf could pick up on it and start to lose his shit.

Rain: Got them to the River doctors. They're hooked up to monitors, but the scent in the air is grim...

Rain: No sign of them waking.

It made sense for them to go to the River pack. Though the Stone wolves were closer, the River pack had far better medical equipment. Who knew what passed for medical treatment for the Stone wolves? They notoriously rejected most modern technology.

Rain had made a tough call.

Not only was the drive farther, putting them at risk for the humans to find them again... Going to the Edgeriver wolf pack effectively cut out all support from the Stonevalley wolves and their supporters.

But it was the only chance that the silver-sick wolves had to make it out of this alive.

My head was still buried in my phone, sorting through all the details of last night,

when I absentmindedly walked back into my room. I was fucking pissed—more at myself than at Rain, or even the humans who'd done this. My adrenaline was pumping so hard that I'd somehow forgotten that the bedroom wasn't empty.

Camille was sitting up in bed, with nothing but a blanket wrapped around her perfect curves.

The moment our eyes met, Camille flinched.

She drew back subtly as the room flooded with the sharp ammonia-like scent of anxiety. My gorgeous, perfect girl was practically shaking, watching me with wide eyes as if she was afraid that I was going to hit her.

What. The. Fuck.

CHAPTER 25
CAMILLE

I was getting too familiar with waking up disoriented. But this time, I wasn't in a cave, in my run-down apartment, or shackled to a gurney.

For a moment I didn't know why I was in a beautifully furnished room, wrapped in the softest sheets I'd ever slept in. The next moment, Roman barged inside, with the scent of his anger swirling so strongly in the air, I was plunged straight into a panic.

What was I supposed to do?

Did I get this all wrong? Was I supposed to leave?

Was it something I did last night? During sex?

Roman held his hands up, like he was showing me that he was unarmed, and slowly sat down on the other side of the wide bed. Giving me space.

Not that it mattered. A wolf his size could lunge across that distance in moments, tearing out my throat.

He might be acting cautiously around me, but the scent of his anger was still there, though it had transformed into something sharper, something controlled—his emotions spiked the air in acid. It was heavy and thick around us as fog.

"Did I hurt you?" Roman's posture was already stiff, but he tensed up even more, as soon as the words were out of his mouth.

But he didn't make any sense. Roman was angry at me? Because he hurt me?

I shook my head sharply.

"Who hurt you? Was it Mike Bowman?"

Shit. He knew about my ex? The way that anger accented each syllable of his name, it was obvious that Roman *knew* the exact nature of the relationship I used to have with Mike.

I shook my head, rapidly, as my heart began to pound in my chest, skittering out of control. No, Mike would never... well, I thought he would never hurt me. At least... he would never hurt me physically. It was part of the reason I fell for him. He was so different from the men in my life. He was supposed to be *safe*.

Which was stupid, because Mike ended up hurting me more than anyone else.

Now my heart was pounding so wildly in my chest, I thought it would break. This wasn't supposed to happen.

Roman was one of the fiercest wolves I'd ever met, but everything in me had told me that he was different from the alphas I'd known. Not aggressive and careless. I couldn't even imagine Roman getting angry enough to slap me around or break my bones. But right now, he was mad enough to *kill* someone.

"Why are you mad at me?" The words slipped out, making me sound worse than weak. I sounded *pathetic*.

I had to stay strong and aloof. I needed to protect myself from pain. Instead, tears were prickling in the corners of my eyes and nothing I could think of could make them stop. Against my wishes, a sole tear trickled down my cheek.

Slowly, like a hunter trying not to scare off his prey, Roman reached over to me. He brushed away the tears, brushing away the sadness left behind in wet trails.

"I'm furious. But not at you." Roman cradled my face in his hands, stroking gently across my cheeks, staring into my eyes like he wanted to memorize me. "I'm furious that you're so terrified, you're almost shaking. Someone's taken their anger out on you before."

The way that he said it, it wasn't a question. It was as if Roman could open up my skull and peer down at that scared little girl I used to be.

"I wasn't there for you when they hurt you, but I'm here now. I promise you that no one is ever going to put their hands on you. I won't let them." He leaned in closer, his voice going low and dangerous. "I'll kill anyone who makes you flinch like that again."

My heart skittered in my chest, like it wanted to leap out of me and embrace him, as my whole face flushed bright red. What do you say to something like that?

But then Roman's gaze shifted down my body, where the blanket slipped out from my grasp in my panic—he had my whole body feeling heated for an entirely different reason. He couldn't tear his eyes away from my bare breasts, as the scent of anger in the room faded, replaced by something thick and seductive—a delicious cocktail of pheromones and lust.

When he managed to force his gaze to meet mine once more, his eyes were half hooded with desire. "Are you sore?"

I bit my lip. The way that he was looking at me was all the healing I needed.

While his cock might be huge, splitting me open harder than the night I'd lost my virginity, there was something about the yearning in Roman's expression that had me desperate for a repeat. Slowly, I shook my head.

"Don't lie to me."

"It's just that I really enjoyed last night. I thought that I couldn't—" I cut myself off, blushing. Oh, Goddess. Why had I almost blurted that right out loud?

"You couldn't what?"

Ugh. Of course, he wouldn't let that go.

I swallowed, trying to loosen whatever it was that was stuck in my throat. Was it pride? Was it my ego, stubbornly clinging on?

"I thought that I couldn't come during sex. Some women can't, until last night I thought that I was one of them..." my voice trailed off, awkwardly, and I had to turn away from the heat in his gaze that had just turned molten.

"You never had an orgasm during sex? Not once?"

"No. Not until last night."

He shook his head, confused. "But I felt you... through the bond."

What? He could feel what? I might as well have the moon goddess strike me now, because I was never going to live this moment down. My mind raced as I went though the last few months after I crashed into Roman, igniting our soulbond.

I forced myself not to groan out loud as I realized exactly *what* he was feeling.

"That was my... vibrator."

There was a possessive glint in Roman's eyes, as his

eyes roamed over mine speculatively. It heated every inch of my skin as scorching as his touch.

In a moment. Roman closed the last bit of the distance between us. He grabbed me by the hips, tugging me so suddenly that I was on my back, flat on the bed, before I could realize what he was doing.

Fuck. Yes.

Screw treating me like I was made of glass. I needed more of him. I needed to make up for all the lost time where I was acting absolutely bat shit crazy. When I *ran* from this delicious morsel of a man.

Roman pressed open-mouthed kisses into my soft inner thighs. The hot press of his mouth against my sensitive flesh burned every thought out of my mind. He reduced me to a whimpering mess that needed *more.*

Every movement of his lips was utter bliss. Every motion, perfection. I didn't figure out where the path of his kisses was heading, until his lush mouth was right *there,* pressed directly against my pussy, his tongue lapping against me, like I had the most delicious cream at my core.

I canted my hips, helplessly writhing against him, arching my back to get more of that delicious friction, completely out of control. Roman squeezed my thighs, holding me in place, right where he wanted me.

He let out a deep groan, before diving in, spearing me with his tongue. That wet slide, the pressure of his hot tongue—he was driving me out of my mind, out of my body, driving me to a place where I was reduced to pure pleasure.

I dug my nails into the silky sheets, needing something to hold on to, something to ground myself. I felt myself being pulled apart at the seams.

Roman knew exactly what I needed. He reached for my

grasping fists and interlaced his fingers with mine—holding on, as my whole body trembled and tensed. My head slammed against the mattress as I clenched my eyes tight, as the tension wound tighter and tighter within me—coiling inside of me until I was shaking with it.

Without warning, I came.

Strong as an electric bolt, it raced up the entire length of my spine, vibrating through each of my limbs in pulsing waves.

I let out a high-pitched shriek as my orgasm ripped through me. Shudders wracked through my whole body as every inch of me was obliterated by its intensity.

I lay there on his silky sheets, utterly lost. Utterly shattered into pieces.

That was...

Holy shit.

No one told me that an orgasm could feel like that...

Roman settled himself next to me on the bed and held me through the aftershocks. He pressed gentle kisses to my temple and rubbed soothing patterns across my arms.

When I finally caught my breath, I turned to him. "You aren't going to fuck me?"

He shook his head, no.

"If it isn't going to feel good for you, then I don't want it."

"Not that I'm complaining, but that doesn't seem fair."

"You've just told me that no lover has ever made you come. That means that you have *years* of orgasms to catch up on... and every single one is going to be because of me. Under my cock, and my fingers and my tongue." Roman pressed a heated kiss against my neck, holding me tighter. "I'm just getting started making sure that you get every last one."

CHAPTER 26
ROMAN

"Roman?"

My mate called me from the main bedroom that was now *our* bedroom. It was good to see her get more confident around me. Camille had been hesitant at first, acting at times like she was trying hard not to upset me—which was ridiculous.

I hadn't managed to pleasure her enough times to show her that she was my everything, that I would do *anything* for her, but this was still new for us.

She'd already gotten comfortable enough to furnish and decorate the unfinished rooms in the house. Turns out, my mate has quite the eye for interior design. Every one of her projects made the house feel more like a home than any of my ideas. Or maybe it had to do with her being here with me. She probably wanted my opinion on something she'd rearranged, or a purchase she was considering.

"I'll be there in a minute, sweetheart." I called after her.

She was the sign I needed to get a move on with the voting.

It was an email that had gone out to all the alphas in

the surrounding territories, seeking multi-pack coopera-tion. I'd sat in the office overthinking for too long already. It was a message regarding the silver-sick wolves. Though the River-pack doctors said that their conditions had stabilized, they'd had no signs of waking. The email was a request to send non-mated shifters to them to see if a soulbond could wake them.

This had the potential to blow up, with so many packs working together. On the one hand, I wanted to give the silver-sick wolves a chance to find their mates—Goddess knows that we couldn't afford to lose more wolves. Obvi-ously, the other alphas needed to be informed of the threat of the human experiments. But on the other hand, having that many dominant wolves in close proximity was a breeding ground for that single moment of disrespect, or the ill-timed hostility that could degrade into another full-fledged war.

Could I imagine what my life would be like, if I never got the chance to have Camille in it?

I clicked 'yes,' before I could talk myself out of it, submitting my support, then went off to find my mate.

As soon as I reached the bedroom, I saw Camille wearing a long trench coat and a mischievous smile. I nudged the door shut with my foot, letting the room fill with the aroma of the two of us mixed together. It was a scent that was quickly becoming my favorite—one that was starting to feel like home. I inhaled deeply, feeling how Camille's scent soothed my wolf, and picked up on the smell of leather in the air. What was—

Camille unknotted the trench coat, slipping it off her shoulders revealing an outfit that short-circuited my brain, erasing every thought from my head.

That was—wow.

Camille was wearing leather lingerie that bound across her breasts in strips, making me painfully aware of all the parts of her I needed. All the remaining blood in my head rushed south as I reached for her, needing to touch her. I needed to drag my tongue across all of that milky skin that her ensemble was showing, and rip the rest *off*.

Camille darted out of my grasp, shaking her head coyly.

Oh? She wanted to play, did she?

Camille circled around me, and I turned slowly, not letting her out of my sight. All of a sudden, she pushed me and I allowed myself to fall on the bed, backing up until I was on the center of the mattress.

Slowly, my mate started to crawl toward me with an expression of pure and feral lust on her beautiful face. I pulled myself upright immediately, ready for her. She bit her lip and shook her head no, and I lay back down. My blood was coursing through my veins and every inch of my body was pulsing with the need to grab her. To take her. Now.

It was official; this girl was trying to kill me and I think that she might be succeeding.

When she finally got to me, Camille started to unbutton my shirt. Fire was lighting across my skin, with each inch she exposed. I cursed myself for wearing a shirt with so many buttons. Seriously, I think I only owned like three button downs. Why did it have to—

My soulmate licked my chest. The wet slide of her tongue felt so fucking good that it took everything in me not to pull her down to the bed and get her under me. My entire body was tense with the need to be inside of her.

I held myself still, letting Camille take the lead. Every inch of me was strained. She kissed a path down my belly, and my muscles bunched under each one of her kisses. Had to force myself not to ruin the moment by grabbing her, bearing down on her and taking control.

Then Camille was at my belt, unbuckling it in moments. Slowly, she drew the zipper all the way down, and by the time her hand reached the bottom, my patience was in tatters, just holding on by a thread. I was already rock hard, and Camille's hand in close proximity to my cock was making my erection so intense that my whole body ached.

As Camille began to finally tug my pants free, I lifted my hips to help her. Now with my boxers off, my cock finally freed and painfully ready, I reached for Camille to return the favor. The only way that lingerie on Camille could look better, was if it was on the floor after I got her completely naked.

She raised her eyebrow at me in warning, and my hand fell back to my side. *Fuck.* She was torturing me.

Tilting her head, Camille placed burning kisses to my sides, to my stomach, to wherever she could reach.

"Camille," her name on my lips was part growl, part curse. More than anything, it was a plea for her to do something to relieve my agony. To help me hang on to the shred of control I still held. I couldn't even blame my wolf for my lack of control. He was laying back within me, enjoying the show. No. My impatience to have her was all on me.

Rising to her knees, Camille straddled me, rubbing her entrance against the tip of my cock. She guided me inside her, then slowly slid down—taking all of me inch by inch. Not stopping until our pelvises were touching and she had taken all of my girth.

I groaned, lost in the sensation.

I'd never allowed anyone to ride me before, and it felt different. Camille was in control of the pace, and with the slow undulations of her hips, I felt every inch of her. I could memorize the exact shape of her pussy this way—all of her silken heat.

I couldn't take my eyes off her as she rocked against me. Her entire body was perfectly on display for me. Every curve on her body moved in sinuous waves.

My whole cock was sheathed in molten pleasure, and every muscle in my abdomen was flooded with tension.

All of my concentration was locked on her—the way her mouth parted in pleasure, the way that her eyes went hazy whenever we moved together just right, and the way that the muscles in her stomach flexed as she rocked her hips against mine.

Slipping one finger right to her clit, I rubbed her firmly with exact pressure and just the right circular motion that I knew would set her off.

I was wired. Addicted to the little gasps that told me she was close. To the way that her rhythm changed as she sought her climax, the way that her movements became harsher, more aggressive.

Then her voice broke as she *moaned*.

My soulmate didn't look real when she came. She was unearthly—a goddess. Her head tipped back in bliss and her gorgeous tits lifted towards the heavens.

Finally, as Camille was distracted by her own orgasm, I gripped her hips tight, and bucked into her delicious pussy. Hard. Like I'd wanted to do the moment that she'd slipped that trench coat off of her shoulders.

Camille had gotten me so riled up that it didn't take me long to finish. With a deep thrust, I came hard. My cock throbbed, releasing cum deep into my mate in thick spurts. Pleasure shot straight from my tight balls, tingling up my spine, and radiating to every limb of my body.

I wrapped my arms around my mate, holding her as

aftershocks of my climax shuddered through me. I rubbed her arms, my touch lingering on her shoulder, on the geometric swirls and constellations marking our soulbond. Pale light fluttered within the mark at my touch.

Fuck. We needed to do that again.

Later today, I was going to buy her three new sets of lingerie and make sure that her closet was packed. But before that, I had to tell her something that I should have told her a long time ago.

I'd done everything wrong when it came to her.

From practically abandoning her, and almost giving up on her... to seeing her get captured and nearly dying at the hands of those fucking pseudo-scientists... Then demanding that she give up her old life to come with me.

But for some reason, she was still here in my arms. Now that she was, I was going to do everything in my power to keep her there. I'd spend the rest of my life making sure that I'd get things right.

"Camille," I waited until her eyes flicked back open, though sleepy and sated.

"I love you."

CHAPTER 27
CAMILLE

"Dance with me." I whispered into the shell of Roman's ears.

With his sharp senses, I didn't need to lean in closer for him to hear me. No, I just used it as an excuse to be near him.

I couldn't get enough of him. I'd use any excuse to get my hands on him. His rock hard muscles under buttery smooth skin—it was everything I needed to feel safe. More than safe—being with him made me feel vibrantly alive. He was warm, and comfortingly solid, like strength personified.

I could feel the connection between us as steady as my heartbeat, and being this close to him made everything feel right in the world.

"For you, anything," Roman murmured back.

On Roman's lips those words were a pledge, vowing that if there was anything I needed, anything at all—he would be there for me.

My mate was a fairly stoic man. It was easier to see him at the front of a battlefield than in the middle of a dance floor, but he strode with me straight into the crowd of dancers.

Honestly, I'd been feeling a bit nervous about tonight. I never thought that I would ever come back to the Howlers' Den. Not after my scandalous departure last time.

Everyone knew that I ran straight from the dance floor after my soulbond sparked, but I doubt that anyone would be stupid enough to mention anything about it. Not with Roman around.

My mate didn't even need to say a word to be the most intimidating alpha in the establishment. His build wasn't the brawniest, but he had an undeniable power to his presence that shifters noticed as easily as a flashing neon sign.

It wasn't as if I was the hottest topic of gossip anymore. Now the only thing everyone could talk about was the experiments on shifters... even the thought of it sent a chill slithering down my spine and phantom pins and needles prickling through the arm they had mangled. It was a big enough threat to our way of life that all of the packs were working together to help the silver-sick wolves who remained unconscious. The River and Blackwood packs tested all of their unbonded wolves and so far just one shifter found their soulmate and was able to wake. In hushed conversation all around us, people wondered who would be next.

I hadn't gone out for a night of fun... since my scandalous departure the last time I was at the Howlers' Den. But as soon as I walked in, I just ended up slipping back into the scene. The music pumping, the smell of alcohol and desire in the air—it was all so familiar.

Then Roman's hands were on my hips, as he slowly swayed to the beat. He had the sinuous grace of a predator.

Every single one of his movements hinted at the strength in his powerful body.

Suddenly, he pulled me closer, until I was pressed against him. Rocking my body along his was as natural as breathing. I was shimmying my shoulders, and swaying my hips, getting lost to the music, to the pull of the beat, and the searing heat of my mate's gaze on me—to this perfect moment.

I still don't believe that it was fate that recognized my ideal partner, but I believed in Roman. I could see for myself the kind of man that he was, and I'd chosen him.

After the song ended, Roman pulled me tighter against him, pressing his lush lips against mine.

His lips were sweeter than honey and dangerous as sin.

The light flicks of his tongue, the warm pressure and delicious friction made all the rest of the world fade away.

Roman leaned in close, so that other shifters would have a hard time picking out what he said over the thrumming beat of the music on the dance floor.

So that his words were just for me.

"If I keep dancing with you, I'm going to want to take you home and fuck you." There was a fire in his eyes that promised to do just that, hot enough for me to want to agree with him... we'd been here long enough. "But we barely just got here, so I'm going downstairs to get us drinks. You want a fruit cocktail?"

The conversation practically gave me whiplash, but the promise of alcohol was enough to keep the human side of me happy... my wolf on the other hand, was pouting right now. She had her nose buried under her paws as she whined.

Down girl. Roman will be naked and ready soon enough, it's time for more dancing.

"Yeah, the watermelon." My voice was high and breathless.

Before he turned away to fetch our drinks, I noted how Roman's lips tugged up in a hint of a smile. My mate knew exactly how much his words could turn me on.

Then the beat dropped on one of my favorite songs. I was swaying in time with the music, ready to bring on the alcohol. To bring on the fun. How had I forgotten how much I loved this?

But now dancing was better than ever. I hadn't realized how much anxiety had clouded the experience of going out before. I had been so terrified of bumping into my soul-mate, or the slim chance that my father would find a reason to track me down and come after me. It was nice to let loose without looking over my shoulder for once. Without those worries hanging over me, nothing could go wrong.

"You have some nerve showing your face here," said a familiar voice.

I felt the exact same sensation in my mind, as if someone ripped a bandaid off straight in my brain, or scratched a record to jolt me out of my good times.

What the?

No. Not familiar.

Though his voice used to be as familiar to me as my own name, now it was nothing but the voice of a stranger.

What was my ex doing here?

"Are you here stalking me?" Mike had a pitying look in his eyes. Once upon a time, I would have told myself that the look on his face meant that he cared. It was only after he had kicked me unceremoniously to the curb that I real-ized that empty words and feelings meant nothing if you didn't have the balls to back it up—to make the words mean something.

Mike could act like he cared all he wanted... but he couldn't even do the bare minimum to be a decent partner. It wasn't that hard not to cheat.

"No," I barely held back from rolling my eyes at him. Honestly, I forgot that he existed. I hadn't even thought of scoping out the dance floor for my ex. I used to come here all the time, and would beg Mike to come with me. It hadn't even occurred to me that he'd show up now.

I was annoyed enough to consider tugging on my bond with Roman. He'd insisted that I practice, in case something were to ever happen. I knew that my mate would come running to my defense... he'd make Mike pay. I know that Roman was just looking for an excuse to put my ex in the ground. It would all end up so messy, and ruin the night.

If I was being perfectly honest with myself, after taking a hard look at Mike now... he wasn't even worth the effort.

It turns out that my ex really did me a favor when he forced me to leave him. I had no concept of how awful our relationship was until I was free from it.

I guess I'd gotten too used to the look of the fierce devotion in my mate's eyes. If anyone hurt someone Roman cared about, he'd burn the earth down to make them pay. My soulmate was loyal down to the *bone*.

Mike had nothing on that.

I guess I'd also gotten used to being around Roman and his generals. My ex was looking downright *shrimpy*. Between Roman and my ex, there was no comparison. It was like a fight between a chihuahua and a cane corso—it barely even made sense that they were still the same animal.

I thought that the two of them had nothing in common at all, until I saw Roman transform into a wolf for the first time. Roman was a sleek, muscular wolf with fur as dark as the night. My ex's wolf couldn't compare, except in fur color—they were both dark wolves.

Why was he even going out of his way to bother me? Did he think that I was devastated without him?

"I'm here with my mate, so..." Mike was staring down his nose at me, like he was dismissing me. Like he was expecting me to bend to his every whim and leave.

It was then, I noticed her. Mike's mate was a pretty little brunette. She was short and slim with dainty features like a pixie. She had been cowering in Mike's shadow, but stepped to her mate's side after he mentioned her. She was clutching on to Mike as if he was some sort of prize, and she was worried that I was here to steal him away from her.

Eww, no.

Besides her unfortunate taste in men, I had no problem with Mike's mate. I wished her well.

She was adorable, with just a tiny hint of a baby bump around her middle that jut out against the stylish black dress... that looked awfully familiar. Too familiar... because it was *mine.*

My nose flared... there was no way. The dress had to be a coincidence. I couldn't believe that she would just have no problem putting on my dress...

But no. There were traces of my scent in the fabric. It was one of the many outfits I couldn't take with me.

A part of me wanted to get heated. It seemed like the two of them shared a common flaw. No one ever told them not to touch what doesn't belong to them. But then again this dress was part of the old life that I'd thrown away. It wasn't worth it to go rooting around in the trash, rummaging after things that I'd already left behind.

Besides, the poor girl was the soulmate to my ex. As far as I was concerned, that was punishment enough.

"Are you done?" My voice was deadpan and I crossed my arms across my chest. Mike wanted a reaction from me and he wasn't going to get it. I wasn't even upset. Dealing with him was just... tedious. "I'm trying to dance here, you're in my way."

Mike's face froze in disbelief.

I raised an eyebrow. Was he always such an ass? If so, why was I only noticing it now? Did he really think that he had the power to make me leave? What was he going to do? Passively aggressively insult me to death?

Mike scowled, raising his voice in a way that was probably meant to scare me. "I don't know what you think you're doing here, but if you think that you can just..."

All of a sudden his face went pale and his jaw snapped shut. Mike wasn't looking at me anymore, but at someone over a foot taller, standing behind me. I didn't need to wonder who could shut my ex down without a word; he was already at my side handing me my favorite drink.

"Keep looking at my mate and I'll take your eye." Roman said with a tone that was deadly calm. The air around us grew tense with the promise of violence. Everything went so quiet around us, I could hear the wolf whimpering pitifully in Mike's chest.

I let the alcohol soothe away the bitter thought that my mate had to come save me again. Closing my eyes, I took a long sip. My drink was crisp and refreshing—the sweetness of watermelon with a perfect kick of alcohol to wash it down. By the time I was done with the first taste of my cocktail, Mike was already halfway to the other side of the dance floor with his pregnant mate trailing behind him.

"Did you hear everything?" I asked.

Roman nodded.

Inside I was cringing. Mike was the dumb mistake I'd made when I was young and hurt. It had happened so long ago, it wasn't fair that my choice should rear his ugly head, embarrassing me to this day.

"You had it handled," Roman shrugged.

Somehow, those simple words of reassurance let out the tension that had jammed up between my shoulders during the conversation with my ex.

"But he's a full grown male who wanted to pick a fight with a woman who isn't his." Roman tipped his glass of dark amber liquor back, draining it in one go. He clenched the glass so hard I was shocked that it didn't shatter to pieces. "No one messes with my mate."

I tipped my own cup to my lips, polishing off the rest of it—letting the bubbly euphoria rise and fizzle in my brain. More than the alcohol, my soulmate's protectiveness was making me giddy. Making me yearn for more than a simple dance. I wanted my limbs to be so tangled up with his that nothing would be able to tear the two of us apart.

"Do you want to get out of here?" I bit my lip, looking up at my man from beneath my eyelashes, so he knew exactly what I meant to do with him as soon as I could get him alone.

Roman took my hand, gently interlacing our fingers.

I walked out of Howlers' Den, listening to the familiar clacking of my heels as I made another quick exit.

But this time I was leaving with the man who held my heart.

About the Author

I'm Miyo Hunter and I'm addicted to Dominant Alphas. Sweet love and dark fantasy. From shifters to omegaverse, I want characters bent over chairs and called a good girl. I want to read until jobs and responsibilities don't exist. Until I'm lost in a world that's spicy and a little bit wild.

If you enjoyed reading, please leave a review. Honest reviews help other readers find books that they may enjoy.

instagram.com/miyohunter
tiktok.com/@miyohunter